C000112901

TO BE CLAIMED

BOOK ONE

WILLOW WINTERS

WALL STREET JOURNAL & USA TODAY BESTSELLING AUTHOR

From *USA Today* best-selling author, Willow Winters, comes a tempting tale of fated love, lust-filled secrets and the beginnings of an epic war.

His chiseled jaw and silver gaze haunts both my nightmares and my dreams, though I've only ever gotten a glimpse of either.

There's a treaty between us and them; mere mortals and the ones who terrify but keep us safe. The contract demands that every year there's an offering and this year I'll walk across that stage presenting myself.
We have no idea what to expect if they choose someone, since they haven't done so in generations.
The only thing we know is that the ones they take belong to them forevermore. If chosen, you don't come back, or so the story of the treaty goes.

Gather and present yourself.
This is the offering ...
... and I ... belong to him.

WOUNDED
KISS

PART I
THE OFFERING

PROLOGUE

Their authoritative presence is felt before anything else. My heart skips a beat and my blood runs cold. *They're here.*

The voluminous cloaks cover their bodies entirely and their faces are mostly concealed by their hoods. Standing with their broad shoulders squared and hands tucked behind their backs, they emanate sheer masculinity and dominance.

His baritone voice whispers, and his breath burns hot against the shell of my ear. His tone is gentle, but there's no doubt in my mind that his words are a command.

GATHER AND PRESENT YOURSELF.
THIS IS THE OFFERING ...

CHAPTER 1

GRACE

I can't stop staring at Lizzie. She's killing it with the look she's going for but the hot pink dress she's wearing is so tight her boobs are nearly popping out. I can't be too mad at her for that—if mine looked that good, I'd put them on display every chance I got. But the hem of her dress ends about an inch below her ass, and that's being generous. *It doesn't leave much to the imagination.* Not that I'm judging. I'm just worried other people will. If she bends over even the slightest, everyone's going to see all her goods. At that image, I scrunch my nose and a thought hits me.

"Are you even wearing underwear?" I try to keep my tone neutral so I don't sound like I'm being a prude, but I can't help asking since she goes commando all the time. Although I can't imagine her risking a wardrobe malfunction considering where we're headed.

She pauses her contouring and shoots me a naughty grin, then rolls her eyes. "Yes." The self-assurance falters in her expression but only for a moment, and I think I may have imagined it. Confidence is practically her middle name.

"Thank God." I breathe out a sigh of relief and watch as she sprays something in her hair and smooths out the ends. Her hands tremble just slightly and this time I know I didn't invent what I saw. "You look hot," I say in an attempt to calm her nerves. It's not the dress that's gotten to her. It's what we have to do the moment we leave that's got her on edge. I know this is true, because it has me shaken too.

"You're just saying that," she says sweetly with a simper that doesn't look at all innocent on her. "It's the blond hair," she adds as she twirls a lock around her finger. "They have more fun."

With only a huff of a laugh in response, I shake my head and ignore the churning in my gut that's been bothering me all day.

She's really nailing the blond bombshell look. Honestly, she pulls off every color she's ever dyed it. Even last summer when she went purple. It looked fantastic on her, like she was made to have violet hair; I would've looked like a complete dumbass.

Touching up my makeup one last time, I stare back at the mirror before smiling and spearing my fingers through my natural brunette hair, giving it more of a relaxed appearance. Lizzie may have the sexy and seductive look down pat, but I've got more of a traditional beauty thing going on. I like my subdued look. It keeps assholes away. Lizzie can handle them, comically so ... I cannot. Smacking my lips, all done with my lip gloss, it's time to decide on shoes.

I'm definitely wearing heels. It's a must when I go out with Lizzie. She practically lives in them since she's short, but so am I. It took me a little while to get used to wearing heels all the time, but now they're like slippers. For tonight, though ... getting all dressed up makes the nerves at the back of my neck prick.

"New jeans?" she asks as she eyes the designer pair I bought the other day. I'm grateful for the distraction. No more thinking about that. The idea of being taken by anyone at all—much less the men who will stand on that stage today— is only a nightmare. It's not going to happen. Not a damn thing is going to happen this afternoon, and then we're *really* going out. That's the plan, and we're sticking to it. I need to stop thinking about the worst things imaginable. Sometimes my mind goes to the darkest places, but not today. Not now. Sure as hell not when Lizzie needs me to be levelheaded.

"Yeah, they're like the best pair I've ever owned." They fit my petite curves better than the rest of the jeans in my closet. I'm rubbing it in a little, but Lizzie knows I'm only teasing. Stretching a little in them, I turn to check out my backside. My curves are on the larger side, but I love it. I've got wide hips and small breasts, whereas Lizzie's got a full-on hourglass figure.

"When'd you get them?"

"Got 'em on sale last week. Should've stayed with me at the mall rather than taking off." I click my tongue at her and smile. She left me hanging when she went to go run an errand for our boss. His lazy ass does that kind of thing constantly. We basically run the bookstore ourselves.

She pouts and asks, "Did they have any more?"

I purse my lips and shake my head. These were the only pair on the clearance rack. If Lizzie and I wore the same size in jeans, I'd share them. But we don't. So she's shit out of luck. "Sorry, babe."

"Damn."

"We'll have to keep a lookout for more." I nod my head.

"We should look online too."

Her eyes shine brightly at the suggestion. "Hell yeah, payday is Friday," she replies in a singsong voice, swaying her head as she does. It makes the dangling earrings she's wearing chime softly. They're rose gold with moonstones. I gave them to her on her eighteenth birthday. Lizzie's allergic to silver, so I made sure to get pure rose gold. They cost a little more, but it was worth every penny to see the look on her face when she opened the gift box. She owns a lot of earrings, but she always seems to wear that specific pair.

The smile grows on my face until I realize I need to ask her the inevitable and it vanishes completely at the thought. "Are you almost ready?" She looks like she is but knowing her, she could spend another hour doing her makeup. I bet she could spend all day in here if I didn't remind her of the time. Her makeup looks perfect already to me, though, with her flawless cat-eye look and pink lipstick to match her dress. "And do you have a jacket?" I add comically, as if I'm her mother.

"Yeah and yeah," she says, rolling her eyes with the smile staying in place, "but we still have time to kill, right?"

I check my phone, which is sitting on the bathroom counter. Our small-town college, Shadow Falls, is only ten minutes away and we have forty minutes before we absolutely need to take off.

Nerves tingle down my arm and my throat tightens. There's not a trace of either when I answer her. "A little bit, yeah." I can guess exactly what it is that she wants. "Coffee run?"

"Yes!" she exclaims to the ceiling with dramatic flair. She's got a serious caffeine addiction. Shaking my head, I smile back at her and grab my phone. I could go for a chocolate chip cookie while we're there anyway. Something to calm my stomach.

"Let's go ... like now ... so we're not late then." I browse through our joint closet, which is crammed full of clothing, for only a split second before picking out my favorite clutch. Taking a moment to admire the pastel plaid print and soft tan leather, I drop in my phone, wallet, and cherry red lip gloss.

"You wearing the pink stilettos?" she asks as if she doesn't already know the answer.

With another smack of my lips, I tell her, "Duh." I wear them almost every day. They're neutral enough that they complement most of my wardrobe but they have a little more pep than nude heels. The dark red soles give them an extra bit of sex appeal, which I love. The additional two inches they grant me doesn't hurt either. It makes me feel like today isn't anything but ordinary and I'm going to kick ass ... just like every other day.

Nothing at all to worry about.

"Unless you need them?" I say, offering them up.

"Nope, it would be too much pink." We're both a size six so at least we can share shoes, even if we can't share clothes. Lizzie has heels in nearly every style and color. She's a girl who likes variety. It's the one thing she really spends money on.

"I swear you never wear any of the others," she says teasingly.

"I like these," I say with a shrug, picking up my pale pink beauties. They make me feel in control and sexy. Why wouldn't I wear them every chance I get?

People say you can grow to hate your best friend when you live together but I can't see that ever happening to us. She's the yin to my yang, the peanut butter to my jelly. More than that, we were both grateful to get out of the shitholes where we grew up. The cherry on top is that we truly love and respect one another.

Always have. Always will.

I first met Lizzie in middle school, only a year after my mom had passed. We were both quiet loners and didn't really bond at first—not with each other, and definitely not with anyone else.

Summertime was when we actually started talking to each other. I approached her first, although I was deathly afraid of being rejected. It was worth the risk because I was more than tired of being so lonely. We were the only girls wearing long sleeves and jeans in the hot weather. That wasn't my first clue, but it was what I needed to sit by her at lunch. I finally gathered the courage to ask her about it, knowing I would be exposing my truth too. Her bruises were from her third set of foster parents and mine were from my father, who was always drugged up, drunk, or just plain angry.

She didn't tell me why she'd begged to leave the previous two foster homes. All I knew was that she was content to remain with the third even though they hit her for no reason. I asked her why she stayed, and she said it was the best she would get. Even as a twelve-year-old I had an idea of what she'd been through and I wasn't okay with any of it being true.

That night we had a sleepover at my house, not that my dad was home and not that her foster parents cared or knew where she was. It was nice to pretend it was a real playdate.

To pretend like we had normal, loving parents who cared about us. I asked her why she'd left the last foster home, but she just shook her head and started to quietly cry. When I thought she was going to let up on the gentle tears that were falling down her face, I leaned in to hug her and she grabbed me fiercely, sobbing hysterically into my chest. Later that night she woke up screaming and I just held her until she fell back asleep. That was almost a decade ago.

Since then, we've been each other's rock.

I grab my keys in the living room and get ready to lock the door to our place. While I wait for Lizzie to grab whatever the hell she's getting, I smile at the sight of our secondhand sofa. Our apartment is finally starting to look like a home. We were able to get jobs at a bookstore after we turned sixteen and as soon as we could afford it, we moved in together. I shake my head, thinking about how we were constantly broke. Between the two of us, we finally had enough saved up just before high school graduation. It's been about a year of us living together in our small one-bedroom studio. I've loved every single second. This is what family is supposed to feel like. Plus we have an amazing shoe collection.

Minutes and more minutes pass of Lizzie not getting her ass to the front door.

"We're not going to be able to get coffee," I yell down the hall, knowing the threat will get her attention.

She shrieks and runs into the room barefoot, shaking out

her blond hair with a huge smile across her face as I laugh. That's the thing I love most about Lizzie. She never lets anything get her down for too long; she refuses not to smile. Without that optimism and without her friendship, I don't know how I would've survived.

She meets me at the front door with a pair of spiked black heels in hand. "Let's do this shit."

CHAPTER 2

GRACE

As we pull into the line at the drive-through for our favorite coffee shop, I can't help but to feel anxious. So much so that my foot on the brake slips and the car jolts. "Shit, sorry."

Lizzie only lets out a short laugh, the worry I feel slightly reflected in her expression.

"What if they take someone this year?" My nerves are getting the best of me now. My tried and true pink heels aren't making me feel a damn bit confident. After we pulled away from our apartment, I could feel my hands growing hot and numb. My breath is coming in shallow and short, and it's starting to give me a headache. Deep, deliberate breathing isn't helping to calm me down; I just can't get rid of this uneasiness. I shake out my hands again and unsuccessfully try to swallow the spiked lump in my throat while Lizzie fidgets next to me.

Not much is known about shifters, not even the werewolves who initially offered us the treaty. The different species stay to themselves, each in their own little group. Intermingling generally ends with a bloodbath and no one wants that. A few books have been published, but they've been proven to be unreliable. A recent news report even said one of the bestsellers on supernatural beings was put out by a vampire as a joke and that it was full of lies. Just thinking of vampires makes my skin crawl. The nonhumans have their own politics and territories, and we have ours.

All of us keep to ourselves ... except for days like these.

These are the shit days, but we don't have much choice. We're weaker. It's as simple as that. Humans have come to rely on treaties for protection. After all, we don't have their natural-born strength and our weapons don't do a thing to hurt them. I've even read about towns that have pacts with vampires, while others have allied with witches. Not in our town, though. Our treaty only applies to the werewolves of Shadow Falls. The other species know it and stay far away. Which I suppose I should be grateful for. I think I would be, if it weren't for the offering they demand.

Every year, Shadow Falls provides an "offering"—it's so fucked up they call it that—for the werewolves. All the women in town between the ages of nineteen and twenty-one have to gather for the shifters and present themselves. It's the law, so we have no choice. Once you're offered, you can't refuse if they choose you. You could leave rather than participate, but that would mean moving to a different town, leaving your family and forgoing the protection provided by the werewolves. My heart races just thinking about all the implications.

Refusing to participate in the rite or not providing an offering would lead to an end of the treaty. It's happened before every few years in various other locales. The news is always quick to cover any protesters who no longer want their treaty. Normally, those who want protection take off as soon as the debates start because they don't want to risk the fallout. Once a treaty is forfeited, all across the country people wait with bated breath to see the repercussions.

The werewolves never attack the towns that break their pacts. The shifters just leave them be. And when the other paranormal and vile creatures of the night show up at the vulnerable homes, there's no one to help. Sometimes it's only days after when people go missing, or worse. Other times it's years. I've watched on the news as fathers cry, begging for their daughters to be returned to them. I've seen pictures of entire towns burned to the ground, supposedly for nothing more than a witch's enjoyment. The attacks themselves are hardly ever captured but the resulting aftermath leaves enough evidence to determine what happened.

Vampires and witches are ruthless, taking without shame or apology. People say there are good ones and bad ones, just like every other species and race. But I've never seen or even heard of a *good deed* done by either vampires or witches. The only silver lining is that although they may wreak havoc, they don't touch what belongs to werewolves. History has proven time and time again that werewolves will win that fight.

It's been nearly one hundred and sixty years since the violence and tragedy that brought about our arrangement with the shifters of Shadow Falls. According to what Lizzie and I were taught in school, vampires came in the night all that time ago and abducted humans to hold captive for their own pleasure, leaving disaster in their wake. At the time the town had no help, no treaty, no one to beg for mercy. Shadow Falls put up a fight as best they could, but it was useless. Families huddled together at night yet in the morning, someone would be gone without a trace. Or they were massacred. Either way, it was hopeless. The vampires would swoop in, drink their fill, and leave their victims to die. Back then, those sharp-fanged villains were careless. Rather than snatching their victims and hiding like they do today, they'd remain on their hunting grounds and flaunt their kills.

It was only a matter of time before the werewolves came. The thick scent of blood that coated the air might have initially attracted them to Shadow Falls but with so many vampires around, the town was ripe for their picking. Desperate and out of options, the mayor at the time begged the werewolves for help. The wolves agreed, but on one condition—Shadow Falls would have to offer their women to them willingly once a year—forever. He agreed without hesitation, knowing there was precedent in forming treaties with shifters, but stopping the slaughter was his priority. Within days the vampires fled, and the ones unlucky enough to get caught by the werewolves were devoured without mercy.

That year, one woman was taken by the shifters at the offering. Since then, the wolves have upheld their end of the bargain to protect the town, but they haven't taken anyone else. Only that one woman at the first offering. She went without a word, without a fight. It's said she went into a trance of sorts and no one ever heard from her again. That's the story we're told and taught, anyway. And that's the reason we're headed to the local college to "offer" ourselves.

This is our first year and we'll have to attend for the next two as well. To put it mildly, I'm freaked the fuck out. I try to remind myself that the shifters haven't taken anyone in a hundred and sixty years. Maybe this is nothing more than an outdated tradition. *How the hell should I know?* But knowing they haven't taken anyone in over a century and a half only drops my fear down a notch, a very small notch.

The fact that I'll be presented to them gives me mixed emotions, but the overriding feeling is complete and utter fear. I finally have a home and safety and a life that I cherish. I don't want to leave. No one really knows what happens if they take you, but it's not hard to guess. If you're chosen, you don't come back. The very idea throws me into full-on panic mode.

With her lips turned down and her gaze looking off to nowhere, I know Lizzie's thinking the same things I am. My hand grips hers as fiercely as she held me that first night she cried in my arms, in my bedroom when we were only kids. "It's going to be fine," I reassure her, surprised my voice is even as the words come out.

A tight smile is my reward, followed by a shrug, then my Lizzie is back. "I'm fine, just … remembering." It takes all my strength to simply nod, pulling ahead in the line for coffee.

Silence brings memories.

We came last year to watch, just to see what it would be like. It was Lizzie's idea. She was far worse than she is now, just being around the werewolves made her tremble.

We nearly left, but we had to know what to expect so we could prepare ourselves. About a hundred girls were lined up single file and in alphabetical order, then they crossed the stage. If I had seen a picture of it and didn't know the context, I would have thought it was a graduation. A snort leaves me at the comparison. Unlike a graduation, the atmosphere was ominous and grim with no speeches or sense of joy. The werewolves came, the women walked in front of them, and then the shifters left. It was somber and perfunctory, almost like neither party wanted to be there. I know for a fact that was true on our end.

Even though the werewolves were mostly covered by their cloaks, it wasn't hard to tell that they were pure muscle. Nothing but killing machines. I couldn't see much from the other side of the stadium but Sherri, one of the cashiers at the bookstore, told me that they looked "scary as fuck," as she so eloquently put it. She's a senior in college now, so her last time to walk was last year. She told us she couldn't be more grateful.

I wondered why all the women walked quickly and quietly with their heads bowed, but I guess that's why. Not that I can blame them. If someone were staring at me like they wanted to rip my throat out—again, Sherri's phrase, not mine—I wouldn't want to look them in the eye either. Especially knowing they could legally take me against my will.

So yes, head down and a fast pace.

"You okay?" Lizzie asks with a bravado I know is fake, but I love her anyway for trying to be strong for us both. Lizzie licks her lips and then pulls out a tube of gloss from her bag. She can barely look me in the eyes.

"Fine. We're going to be just fine." I pat her hand before pulling up to get our drinks and then taking off. Time to face the music, so to speak.

"Of course we are." She smacks her lips after applying a thin, glittery coat of gloss but I notice how her hand trembles. "And then we're going to whoop it up at Jake's party." I force a small smile for her and try to shake off my nervousness. If not for me, then for her. At least I'm concentrating on the party tonight instead of the offering. Arriving at the college a few minutes later, we park in the designated spots for "those participating in the offering." I turn off the car and grab my stuff from the back seat, keeping my snide thoughts to myself.

"You think Mike's going to be there?" she asks as she opens her door. I follow her lead and walk quickly with her to the stadium entrance, trying to figure out what she's even asking. Right. Jake's party. We only have a few minutes left to get in there for the offering. If you don't make it, you're forced to leave town. *Supposedly.* No one ever risks being kicked out of a protected area, so I don't really know if that particular law would be enforced. Not that I have any intention of finding out firsthand.

"He told me he would." She's been trying to decide whether or not she wants to make a move on Mike. I don't think she should. He keeps coming into the bookstore just to flirt with her and never buys a book. He's worked at his father's construction company since last year when we all graduated. Whenever I suggest he buy something, he always tells me he has no need for any books, not that he has any time to read. He could use a book, though. He's kind of an ass and she deserves way better than him.

"Do you really have the hots for Mike?" I question, not bothering to hide my disdain. I'm all for blue-collar guys. Just thinking of those rough hands on me sends shivers across my shoulders in a good way. I'm just not into assholes. And Mike is way more ass than he is anything else. A shrug is all I get in reply while we both sign our names at the check-in station. After we're each handed a pamphlet, we make our way up the steel steps to sit in the back. I toss the handout into the trash as we walk. It's full of facts about Shadow Falls and how the treaty was formed. I read it last year and I'm not really a history type of girl. Even if I was, that's not the history I want to read about. It's basically designed to sugarcoat the one unquestionable requirement from the wolves. If you're chosen, you must leave with them that instant. No packing your things, no saying goodbye to friends and family. They take you. Plain and simple. I don't need a pretty piece of paper to brighten up that bit of information.

"I really want to get my cherry popped before college." The absurd statement brings me back to the present.

My gaze shoots over to Lizzie. She's practically the only virgin I know. I wonder if she told me because she's looking for a major distraction right now since we'll have to line up soon. Even if she's not, I am, so I'll run with it.

We decided to only take a year off of school between high school and college to save up money, so that means she'd only have a few months to lose it. *If* she's serious.

"For real?" I can't help but to question her. She's never shown any interest before. She nods her head, but it's quickly followed by a bite of her lip. I know she wants my approval. Not that I'm an expert or anything, but I'm far more comfortable with sex.

"Why?" I ask in all sincerity. "It's really not what people make it out to be." We take our seats and stare at the empty stage as Mr. Horga, the gray-haired mayor of Shadow Falls, makes his way across the field with a wireless microphone. "Seriously, I have a better time with my vibrator." She laughs at me and goes back to sucking down her drink.

"I just feel like such an outcast, you know?"

"Yeah, I know how you feel." We've always been two peas in a pod, dancing to a different beat than everyone else. I clasp her hand with the intention of talking her out of pursuing Mike, but suddenly the whole stadium goes quiet as our gazes are involuntarily pulled to the entrance, waiting for the shifters to walk in and show themselves. Their authoritative presence is felt before anything else. My heart skips a beat and my blood runs cold. It's overwhelming. I swallow thickly. *They're here.*

"Oh shit," Lizzie hisses in a low whisper. She dropped her drink and what little bit was left is all over the floor in front of us. Her hands are shaking even harder now. "Sorry," she whispers and half the people around us give her a wary glance before turning back to the cloaked werewolves who are striding across the field toward the stage.

"Just come here," I say, begging her as if she's running away when she's still right here next to me.

"Did it get on your heels?" I look at her like she's lost her damn mind, silently willing her to be quiet, but when I look at her as she tries to clean up the mess, her expression is distressed.

"It didn't get me," I say quietly, focused on easing her worry. I wish I had something to help her wipe up the spilled coffee, though. She's only got the one tiny napkin that was wrapped around the cup so it's already soaked and useless. I give in and laugh a little bit before I look back up, which at least makes her grin in response. Her smile makes me feel like we're okay. Only seconds later, my own vanishes and my heart sinks. I try to swallow but my throat closes as three of the werewolves turn their heads in our direction. Their gaze on us feels like a cold blanket draped over my shoulders and my mouth goes dry. *Fuck.*

"All right, that's better." Lizzie's comment breaks the spell. I let out a small breath of relief when I realize she didn't notice the werewolves staring our way.

I reach for her hand and it feels hot in mine.

"Hey love, you're all right," I say to her.

She tells me back the same. It's what we've done for years when we're scared. Her voice is calmer and more comforting than mine. She doesn't seem to give a shit about their presence, which does wonders for my nerves. Thank God she's being strong when I can't. She squeezes my hand tight and smiles brightly at me. "We're going to walk up there then walk right back down." I force a small smile on my face and nod my head. Up and right back down. It almost sounds simple when she puts it like that.

"Head down," I add for good measure.

I look back at the four men who are now on stage, standing in a row. The voluminous cloaks cover their bodies entirely and their faces are mostly concealed by their hoods. Standing with their broad shoulders squared and hands tucked behind their backs, they emanate sheer masculinity and dominance. I breathe out deep.

"I got you, babe." She kisses the back of my hand, but doesn't release it. It's a good thing too because I don't plan on letting go either.

Mr. Horga has started calling out names. Lizzie and I make sure to go to the back of the line since both our last names start with W. We're dead last except for one older girl, a girl I recognize from school—I think she was two years ahead of us—who has the most vibrant red hair I've ever seen. She's supposed to be in between Lizzie and me. We've never spoken to her before, only seen her around school but this redhead isn't very talkative so we just keep to ourselves. Even though she keeps staring at our clasped hands like she's desperate to take her place in between us, I plan on waiting till the last second to get behind her. I'll be the final person to walk on the stage. My anxiety skyrockets.

"I wonder what they look like." Lizzie's curiosity knows no bounds, even if her voice is shaky. At this moment I couldn't possibly be more grateful for the diversion and I'm damn sure to ignore the tremor in her tone. I need something to get me out of my head and so does she.

"We're just going to be able to see their faces, and that's only if you look directly at them. Which you should not." I mutter my response. I'm not that bold. Glancing to the stage ahead of us, I see about half the girls have already filed through. Some of them approach confidently but all of them walk down the steps at the other end with their heads bowed, eyes glued to their feet. The stage is so long that there are at least ten girls on it at a time. The four shifters are spread out so that you're never more than a few feet away from one. They're just standing there like statues, not moving or saying anything. A chill runs down my spine. I'm no coward, but I plan on keeping my gaze down the entire time.

I can't stand how tense it is, so I blurt out the first thing that comes to mind. "Sherri said they all have a stick up their ass." We're getting closer to the stage and I swear my heart's trying to leap out of my chest and escape. Swallowing is useless; my throat is suddenly dry.

"Do their faces look different from ours?" the girl who's trying to get between us asks.

"I don't think so." I manage to get that out but then my chest starts heaving frantically as I see how close to the stairs we are. Lizzie finally takes her eyes away from the stage and places her hands on my shoulders while we continue to move forward

"You're all right, babe," she says reassuringly. "Now tell me the same."

"We're fine, Lizzie. Nothing bad is going to happen to you, or to me. I promise." I do a quick count and there are only four women ahead of us now.

"I love you, Lizzie." Tears start welling up in my eyes. I have to tell her. Just in case.

Now there are three.

"We're not saying goodbye," she whispers, sounding hopeful and I nod.

Only two ahead of us now.

"I love you too." She kisses my cheek as her name is called. I finally let go of her hand and immediately feel the loss.

Now one.

Breathe.

Miss Redhead walks up.

Breathe.

My name is finally called, marking the end of this year's offering. It's so close to being over. Just a few steps and it's done.

Although I hear my name ringing in my ears, my body falters and my fingers and toes go numb. I force my shaky legs up the four steps and try to control my breathing. Licking at my dry lips, I grip the clutch dangling from my wrist tight in my hands like it can protect me. My heels make loud clicks on the metal stage as I walk, and I concentrate on the sound. I remind myself that I just need to take one step at a time and then it will all be over.

As I let out a small breath at the calming thought, three things happen at once: the werewolf I just passed starts walking off the stage, I feel a large hand on my back, and I hear Lizzie scream. My eyes shoot up to locate Lizzie but before I can run to her I'm pulled against a hard chest by a strong arm made of corded muscle. I'm held firmly in place as a scream tears up my throat. My fingers frantically work to pull the werewolf off of me, my nails digging into the large hand splayed across my belly, but it's useless.

She's still screaming, and I can't even look at whoever's holding me, I can only stare as Lizzie struggles to free herself. "Somebody help her!" I scream. Slamming my elbow against the wall of solid muscle behind me doesn't do a damn thing. Panic turns my skin hot and chaos whirls around me. With all my strength I shove my weight forward, once again pushing away from the beast holding me while shouting her name.

"Lizzie!" I shout as my feet fly off the ground. The shifter restraining me has one arm wrapped around my waist, lifting me up as though I weigh nothing at all. His other hand cups the side of my head, bringing my ear to his lips. The forceful move makes my entire being instantly still.

"Calm her down," his baritone voice whispers, and his breath burns hot against the shell of my ear. His tone is gentle, but there's no doubt in my mind that his words are a command. My mind finally registers what he's said and I take in the scene as if in slow motion. The stage is now empty except for the shifter holding Lizzie, who's fighting like crazy with tears streaming down her red face, and me. Blocking the stairs on either side of the stage are the other two shifters, who act as guards.

Not a soul in the crowded stadium is moving from their position in the least. No one is coming to help her. It's only me. The only humans even remotely close to us are Mr. Horga, who's on the grass where I was just standing moments ago, an expression of complete shock etched on his face, and Miss Redhead. She's huddled in a ball on the side of the stage where she's been allowed to go and venture off. Everyone is silent from both terror and surprise while Lizzie is shrieking and crying, held tightly to the mammoth shifter's chest. Her fists beat against him, not doing any good, but the werewolf allows it, making no move to stop her. It's useless and he lets her waste her strength.

After repeating his command, I'm slowly released by the beast of a man holding me. I nod and the tears that had gathered in the corners of my eyes slowly trickle down my face while quiet sobs rock my body. Not Lizzie. Not my best friend. *They can't take her.* The realization finally hits me as I'm lowered. *They're taking Lizzie.* As soon as my stilettos touch the ground, I dart over to her, the trance broken. I wrap my arms around the part of her torso I'm able to reach, the part not restrained.

It's surreal. I would give anything in the world to deny that this is happening. That it's only a nightmare. The glare behind me sinks deep into my back and I remember his wish: calm her down.

"Lizzie!" I have to shout at the top of my lungs for her to hear me. When she doesn't respond, I yell her name again. It doesn't stop the wretchedness that wreaks havoc inside of me.

"Lizzie!" She stops shrieking for a moment and looks at me with frightened, glossy eyes as she grabs me with the half embrace that she can manage, yet with such force that I'm surprised I don't fall over. As soon as she's quiet, stifling her sobs in the crook of my neck, the shifter holding her gently places her feet on the ground. She nearly collapses as her spiked black heels scrabble to find purchase on the stage. I'm vaguely aware that the people watching us are a mix of emotions. Some are crying, while others have started screaming. But all I can really focus on are Lizzie's whimpers.

A force flows through me; I need to try and say something to calm her. It's like a wave, but I stop it. My body stiffens as I feel the werewolf from earlier approach me from behind. His hand comes down and lands on my shoulder. At first he squeezes firmly, causing me to go rigid, but then his hold loosens and his thumb starts rubbing soothing circles against my nape. I blink away the haze of fear and confusion to look up past Lizzie, who still has her head buried in the crook of my neck. She hasn't stopped crying hysterically.

It's okay, I say. The words rush out of me even though I know it's a lie. My breath is warm in the air between us and my heart pounds in my chest so hard I can hardly hear myself.

I hold her tighter when I see the face of the werewolf behind her. He's staring at me with darkness in his eyes, like I've stolen his prey. I suppose that's exactly what I've done. His chiseled jaw is covered with dark brown stubble and his narrowed eyes are silver, but beyond that he looks human. He would look utterly breathtaking if he could turn his scowl into something less menacing. At his stern expression I take a step back, survival instincts warning me to take flight, but I'm prevented from escaping by the shifter holding me tight from behind. *We're trapped.* Lizzie looks up at me when I flinch at the thought. My eyes dart from hers to the silver stare of the wolf behind her. My body goes rigid as two hands grip my hips to steady me.

"Follow him and bring her with you," the dominating man behind me whispers and again I feel his hot breath tickle my neck as his lips brush against my ear. He releases me without another word and I try to walk while supporting the bulk of Lizzie's weight. We stumble and I almost fall, but the strong hands behind me reach out to steady us before forcing me forward. My chest heaves and my body shakes when I realize I'm going to lose Lizzie forever. They're using me to calm her down and lead her to some unknown fate.

"No," I whisper in defiance. "You can't take her." I try

to protest, but the hand is strong and then something else, something I'm not able to fight, grips ahold of me.

My breathing falters and I immediately feel light-headed. I can't. I can't do that to her.

The last thing I hear before my vision goes black is Lizzie's scream.

CHAPTER 3

GRACE

Waking up with a pillow under my head and a soft, warm blanket around me isn't what I expect when my eyes shoot open. Part of me believes it was all a nightmare until the reality pieces itself together around me. The rumbling of a car is my first clue and with the fine leather under my hand, I know I must be lying across the back seat. After a moment I ascertain that it's moving fairly quickly and I'm alone in the back of whatever—and whoever's—vehicle this is. Opening my eyes warily to chance a peek at my surroundings proves that I'm right.

No! My heart races and I can barely breathe.

"I bet he's pissed," a darkly spoken voice says in a

hushed whisper.

"About not being in this car?" another male voice answers. There's a pause and then he continues. "The other one hurt herself. He had to stay with her."

Lizzie. Scrambling to keep still and not panic, I try to recount everything. *No, she can't be hurt, she can't be.* The need to scream out her name is suffocating as I choke on the syllables.

"Do you really think we should have split them up?" a gruff voice asks more casually from the front seat after a quiet moment. I go completely still at the sound. The other man merely snorts in response. Inwardly, I know I need to get a grip. *They took me.* My heart races. *Where's Lizzie? She can't be hurt. Please don't let her be hurt.* Tears prick at my eyes, but I will them away. I don't want the men to hear me crying. I need to be quiet.

"Fuck no we shouldn't have split them up." They both let out low, rough chuckles. My body shakes and it takes everything in me to stay still.

"At least we got the calm one."

"I hope she stays that way. They'll be settled in a bit and everything will be just fine."

Through barely opened eyes, I watch the dark figure in the passenger seat nod his head.

"You hear that back there?" My gut wrenches and my breath halts in my lungs. My eyes widen but I instantly shut them and pretend to still be asleep.

"Your heart's pounding so loud that I'm sure everyone in the car behind us can hear it, Grace." More rough chuckles follow this statement. I swallow and my sore throat protests the movement. My nails scratch slowly on the seat. They speak as if it's all a joke. Anger mixes in with the fear but still, terror overrides everything.

I reluctantly open my eyes and the man in the passenger seat looks back at me. I open my mouth to speak, but the only thing I can say comes out as a whisper. "Lizzie?" There's a pleading in my voice that's undeniable and I hate it, but I wouldn't change it.

"She's fine. She's in the car behind us with our Alpha. He had to calm her down when none of us could. You have a strong friend." The man looks at me kindly while he answers me in a reassuring voice. No, not man. The werewolf. I must look ridiculous to him, huddled under the blanket. I grip the fuzzy fabric tighter and break eye contact to stare at the floor.

It's been a while since I've felt like this, lonely and scared. Helpless and terrified. A while ... but I remember how to deal with it. If I got through that, I'll damn sure get through this.

"I'm going to see my friend again?" I question in a staggered breath and then quickly add, "Soon?"

"Of course," he says. The answer is immediate, and relief weakens every bit of me. I struggle to keep it together as he continues, "I was going to sit back there with you, but I thought you might like some space." His tone is light, bordering on friendly. When his stare doesn't let up, I give a small, hesitant nod in agreement. Gratitude is a funny thing to be feeling at the moment.

"Thought so." He shifts in his seat, but from my periphery I can tell he's still watching me. If I wasn't so terrified, I could think. I could make a plan. As it is, I'm entirely numb.

"You must have some questions." This time it's the driver who speaks.

My heart beats once, then twice as the moment passes in silence. "Who are you?" Both of them laugh. Their relaxed manner calms me, if only slightly. If they plan on killing us, they're quite kind to their prey.

"I'm Lev," the behemoth riding shotgun answers with a wide smile, "and this is Jude." No matter how friendly he aims to be, his sheer size is chilling. With a quick motion to the driver, he goes quiet again but offers me a charming, yet tight-lipped smile. I nod my head again and look back at him steadily. Their easygoing manner alleviates my worry a bit more. I sit up ever so slowly, moving against the wishes of my racing heart and letting the blanket drop to my waist.

If they're going to play this game, this version where everything is just fine, I'll play along. Right up until they give me my friend back and pull the hell over so we can get back home. Somewhere deep inside me, I remember I have a backbone. I didn't fight this hard so early in life to have these assholes destroy it all. Whatever it is they're after, we'll give them something else. I'll find a way. I always do.

"Are you comfortable?" the first one, Lev, asks.

It's only then that I realize the cloaks are gone and the shifter staring back at me is gorgeous. Like the other werewolves, he has silver eyes, but he doesn't look like the shifter who held on to Lizzie back at the stadium. He doesn't possess nearly as hard of a look as her captor did. My heart races as my palms turn clammy at the memory.

"I'm fine," I say although my answer doesn't come out nearly as strong as I'd like. "Is Lizzie okay?"

"She's all right. Just scared." His answer is dampened by something and my stare implores him for more, but he gives me nothing.

Lev has a short beard and his dark hair is long enough to grab at the top, but short on the sides. It also looks like he's had his nose broken at least once, but the bit of imperfection on his otherwise classically handsome face only adds to his masculine appeal. I scoot around in my seat so I can get a good look at Jude. His black hair is short and he's clean-shaven. But I can't see much else of his face other than his full lips.

If it wasn't for their silver eyes and large shoulders, I'd question if they were even werewolves.

Their heads nearly touch the ceiling, and their broad frames look completely out of place in the car. It reminds me of sardines stuffed in a tin. They can't be comfortable. The two of them are almost polar opposites in the vibes they're giving off. Lev could easily be a badass biker and Jude a clean-cut military soldier. But they're not, they're werewolves. I can't let myself forget that, not even for a second.

"Are you all this big?" The question pops out of my mouth without conscious consent. Blaming it on passing out earlier and this odd light-headedness that won't quit, I let my head fall back and try to get my balance.

Lev's slow grin is sexy as hell as he says, "That's what they all ask and—"

Before he can finish, Jude lands a hard blow with his fist against Lev's chest.

"Shut it." Lev's only reaction is a deep, low chuckle that makes his entire upper body, and the entire vehicle, shake.

"I'm sure she's got a better sense of humor than you," he says and grins at me. "Did you want to hear the rest?"

My lips part, but words don't come out. I feel like I'm on the edge of losing it. "I'm not okay." The words are pulled from me and I hate that I spoke the sentiment aloud. The tears that prick my eyes and the coldness around me ... I hate that even more. This isn't real.

"Ah, shit." Lev runs his hands through his hair and then looks back at me apologetically. "You all right?" His face is the epitome of concern and his silver eyes shine with sincerity. It's been absolutely insane since we got to the stadium earlier and his kindness is my undoing. Ugly sobs start pouring out of me as I shake my head wildly. This isn't real at all. I wish I could just wake up.

Terror cloaks my whisper. "I'm not okay."

"Fuck." Lev turns and somehow manages to maneuver his massive body between the two front seats to join me in the back. I immediately feel claustrophobic as my personal space dwindles to nothing.

"This is worse," I blurt out, my response immediate as I shove a palm against his massive chest.

"I'm just going to hold you, okay?" Lev has his arms up but doesn't move them, waiting for me to respond. His voice is calm and his arms look so welcoming that I can't help but nod my head. His muscular arms wrap tight around me, practically consuming my body and making me feel like a small, scared child. I let go of my inhibitions and scoot closer to him, burying my head in his broad chest. Every ounce of him is pure muscle, so he's hard as hell. But at least he's warm and the gentle strokes up and down my back are soothing.

It takes a while with the rumbling of the car and the quiet drive, but I slowly feel myself calm down. Pulling my face away from him, I note the mascara smeared all over the white T-shirt stretched taut across his chest. Inwardly I cringe, but my breathing relaxes as I look up into his silver eyes and then back down immediately. Jude calmly tells me, "You're going to be all right, I promise." And Lev agrees, "You're going to be just fine." Their words and actions put me at ease. I must be in shock. There's no other explanation. The realization wakes me up, sobriety heightening my anxiety once again.

Lev's sharp silver eyes never turn from me when he asks "You all right?" Without looking up or back at him, I nod slightly, biting my lip as I tuck a loose strand of hair behind my ear. I breathe in deep before I turn to stare out the window. There's nothing to look at but trees. I continue to nervously bite my lip. "Where are you taking us?" I question without having the balls to look either of them in the eyes. My heart gallops and the pitter-patter is almost too much. I feel like I'm going to faint. They're silent and neither seems to make an attempt to answer.

"Did you drug me?"

The quick no is followed by a sharp intake of breath and then he says, "We didn't drug you."

Up and down, my nerves climb and fall. All I can do is shove my hands between my thighs to keep them from trembling.

Lev's hand lands on my arm gently, just to get my attention. "I'm sorry. I really am. I'm not going to hurt you. I promise. No one is." I finally look at him. His brows are raised and his lips slightly parted. He looks as though he's trying to coax a wounded animal out from under a car or something. I nod my head and steel myself to ask the only question that matters right now.

"Why did you take us?" His silver gaze takes me in briefly and then his eyes shoot to Jude's in the rearview mirror. Jude is silent and Lev purses his lips. My breathing hitches at their hesitation.

"Well, I didn't personally take you." That's the only answer Lev finally gives me, placing his hand against his massive chest for emphasis. Jude snorts in the front and then shakes his head.

Anger creeps up, causing a deep crease in my forehead as my brow furrows.

Jude asks, "We heard your friend call you Grace. Is it okay if we call you that?"

"Yeah, that's fine." I'm surprised by how sturdy my voice is.

"Okay, Grace," Jude starts, "our Alpha is the one who ..." he hesitates and glances out the rear windshield before looking straight ahead again. "Um."

"Grabbed me?" I say to complete his sentence. My shoulders stiffen at the memory of their Alpha's hands on me. His thumb rubbing soothing circles on my neck as he commanded me to calm Lizzie down. With how tight my throat is, I don't know how I'm breathing.

There's no time for niceties. I need information. That's how we'll survive. It's how I'll save both myself and Lizzie. The constant thump in my chest reminds me of that. I eye Lev who's sitting back, taking up all of the room back here while watching me with an amused expression kicking up his lips.

"Yeah, grabbed you." Jude swallows hard and glances over his shoulder to the car behind us again. Lizzie's in that car. I know she is. She's safe. I'm safe. I'll figure out a way for us to be safe. I will. I'll be damned if I let anything happen to either of us.

"Okay." I drawl out the word in an effort to get him to continue. He clicks his tongue and meets my eyes in the rearview.

"He doesn't want me to talk to you about this, Grace."

"Why not?" I can't help getting pissed. I need to know. "I deserve to know."

"He wants to tell you himself." I let that sink in for a second before realizing their Alpha must have been at the offering if he's the one who grabbed me. Why take me and then ride in a different car in that case? A frown pulls at my lips and my hands fist in my lap. I don't have time to wait.

"Why isn't he riding with me if he took me?"

"Because of your friend, Lizzie," he says and my heart stops at the mention of her name.

"You said she was all right," I blurt out, cutting him off as I lean forward in my seat a bit to get closer to him. It's foolish, I know it is, but I can't help the note of anger that creeps into my tone at the end. I need to be calm; I know that much. Play along, get information. I can't let my temper get the best of the situation.

"She's fine. Don't worry," Lev reassures me, gently pushing me back against the seat. "Devin wants you to put your seatbelt on."

I stare at him like he's gone mad and snort. *Is he fucking kidding?* "Who the hell is Devin?" I don't care that my voice is raised. Completely ignoring Lev now, my head whips back to Jude. With quickened breaths and a tight throat, I say, "And what was that you were starting to say about Lizzie?" So much for keeping my calm ...

"Lizzie's perfectly fine, but she was extremely upset and got a bit physical with us after you passed out." I nod my head. That sounds just like her.

"But she's okay?" There's a threat hidden in my cadence. It's unmistakable and judging by their expressions, they don't miss it.

"She's all right, but that's why Devin, our Alpha, stayed with her and her ... guards." His eyes exchange a glance with Lev's in the rearview again. "To calm them down."

Guards? Calm them down? Rubbing my clammy palms against my thighs doesn't help to keep my head from spinning. I feel like I'm going to snap. I've lost all sense of sanity.

"Let me help you with your seatbelt." Lev tries to push me back against the seat, but I'm still worried about Lizzie and I don't want to just blindly do what they say. Anxiousness wreaks havoc in my mind and I'm getting increasingly upset with how secretive they're being. I push back against Lev's muscular arms, although I may as well be pushing on a brick wall.

"I don't want to wear it." I'm aware I sound like a petulant child but I'm losing it, quickly spiraling downward. I need something to grip onto. *I need Lizzie.* He looks like he wants to say something, but he clamps his mouth shut. "How exactly did he 'calm her down?'" I stare into Lev's eyes, urging him to answer me.

Finally, he says, "He really wants you to wear your seatbelt."

Motherfucker!

Staring down the beast of a man who, I do acknowledge is being kind at the very least, I bite back, "Well, Devin's not here, is he? So he can shove what he wants up his ass." Jude's loud laugh startles me and Lev covers his mouth with the back of his hand as he fakes a cough in an effort to hide his growing smile.

"Let me tell you a secret about werewolves, Grace." Jude pipes up from the front seat sounding very happy with himself. "As long as we're within a few miles of each other and concentrate, we can hear what the others are thinking and saying." I suck in a sharp breath and scrunch my nose. That's not something I've ever heard or read before, but I guess he did say it was a secret.

The car slows down, and the brakes slightly screech as the blur of trees lessens. Goosebumps spread across my skin and prick their way up the back of my neck.

Jude pulls over to the side of the dirt road and stops. *Thump, thump.* The beating quickens in my chest. I look over my shoulder through the back window to see the car that's been following ours pull up behind us. *Fuck.*

I bite the inside of my cheek and ask, "Does that mean he

can hear me too?" *This is good*, I try to convince myself, giving myself a pep talk although my body is on fire with fear.

"Well no, he can't *hear* you," Jude starts as he puts the car in park and twists his body so he can look back at me. "But he can tell what we're thinking about what you're saying." I start to panic at the realization that the Alpha knows I disrespected him. That's probably like telling a mob don to fuck off.

Fuck. Fuckity fuck. My lungs still and I look everywhere around us to find no one moving yet. Maybe I should have just shut the hell up. My temper shouldn't be getting the best of me. My head spins with fear and desperation, my gaze shooting to the handle on the car door.

"Why ..." I want to ask why we pulled over since we seem to be in the middle of nowhere, but the words are stuck in my throat. Lev opens his door and gets out first, allowing a gust of cool air to filter into the car. My body starts to shake. Bracing his hands on the roof, he leans his head into the car and smiles at me.

"Relax, Grace, we're just switching people around. We're only a few minutes away, but Devin thinks it's best that you see him now."

I don't move. I don't say anything as the heavy footsteps come quicker than I'm prepared for.

Devin's faster than I can imagine. There wasn't a moment for me to will my body to move or to run. The car tilts slightly as he climbs into the seat next to me. His masculine, woodsy scent drifts into my lungs and suffocates every thought. He's tall, his jaw sharp and every inch of his corded muscles are showing with his sleeves rolled up. My chest rises and falls chaotically.

"You'll be quiet until we get home."

It's all he says, the words spoken in a deep low tone and anger pulses inside of me, but something else takes over with a force I can't describe.

"I'm scared," I say, whispering the truth although it's not for the same reasons I've been terrified throughout the day … this is something completely different. As if my body, even my soul, knows my life has been irrevocably changed simply because this man looked my way.

"Don't be," he responds and that's when his gaze meets mine for the first time. It's sharp and silver and all-consuming.

CHAPTER 4

DEVIN

Shove what I want up my ass? I kept my face emotionless in front of my pack, but I couldn't help smiling on my way over to her car. I'm glad she's feisty. My mate, my Grace. I love the way her name sounds on my tongue.

I stare at my mate from the corner of my eye. My mate is Alpha as fuck; the powerful force is rolling off of her gorgeous body in waves. If I was a lesser wolf, I'd feel the need to bow to her. It's unbelievably sexy and entirely unexpected from a human. She's subdued, though. At the realization, my grin vanishes and the impassive mask returns. Something's beaten down her Alpha, and I'm going to find out exactly what happened.

At least she's better off than her friend. Calmer, more in

control. Something's very wrong with Elizabeth. I was two seconds away from putting her friend in the trunk. It really would've been for the best. She won't stop calling out for my mate and fighting, which is only causing her to hurt herself. But Dom wouldn't have enjoyed that. Caleb wouldn't have liked it either. I feel so fucking sorry for my betas. Having to share your mate ... that's a problem I'm not sure how to solve. Dom's already fighting an uphill battle. Liz denied him. Screamed at him, pushed him away and beat him repeatedly. It's unheard of for a mate to react that way. She didn't gentle in his arms like my mate did for me. Grace only pushed away from me to get to her friend, her pack. That's what an Alpha does. A chill runs down my spine; that better have been the *only* reason she pushed away.

Dom shouldn't worry, though. Liz's heat will come soon enough and she'll be begging for him ... or Caleb. It's a damn mess. I'm going to have to figure something out before they kill each other.

The headaches don't stop there. Vince felt his mate in the stadium, just like I felt Grace last year. It's going to be hell keeping him off human territory. I should know.

In the meantime, I can't even tell Grace she's my mate. If I did, then Dom and Caleb would have to come up with a way to tell Elizabeth, or Lizzie rather, that she belongs to both of them. And that can't happen until they figure out their shit.

With the strongest members of my pack distracted over

their mates, I should be concerned about us being prepared for the inevitable fallout from my old pack, but all I can think about is Grace. She'll be going into heat soon; I can smell it coming on and I can see it in the flush of her skin. All I need to do is get her alone.

PART II
THE ALPHA

CHAPTER 5

GRACE

"What do you know about werewolves?" Devin, the Alpha, looks at me expectantly, his sharp silver eyes penetrating mine. His intense stare makes my heart beat chaotically. There's an overwhelming feeling of power radiating off of him. His elbow is planted on his large maple desk with his chin resting on his fist. Devin's dark brunette hair has a messy look to it that's sexy as fuck and his five o'clock shadow is begging me to rub against it. I imagine how his stubble would feel against my inner thighs while he laps at my clit, sucking it into his mouth and letting it go with a *pop*. I clench my thighs and swallow thickly in an attempt to suppress these sudden urges. *What the fuck is going on with me?* Devin's gaze heats as a knowing grin pulls at the corners of his mouth. I purse my lips in response to his arrogance.

He brought me in here to his office as soon as the car stopped, practically dragging me away before Lizzie was allowed out of the car. I was only permitted to see her from a distance, her red-rimmed eyes staring back at me with her palm pressed against the window. My heart is a shattered mess.

I didn't want to be separated from her; she's a complete wreck. She shouldn't be on her own. Or left alone with *them*. Devin promised that if I behave and listen, we'll be reunited and left alone to process everything. It killed me to turn my back to her, to obey this werewolf.

But I pray I'm doing the right thing. Minding what he has to say, following his commands.

And that's how I ended up here.

The size of this "office" is ridiculous. It's larger than our entire apartment. I'm in awe of the sheer size and luxury of the werewolves' estate. I assumed werewolves lived in the woods, hunting down animals in their wolf form and basically behaving like savages. If it wasn't for their large frames and silver eyes, I'd have had no idea that these men were anything other than human. Not that I'd ever met a werewolf before. But I'd always imagined them to be ... primitive. And nothing about them or this place is primitive.

If what Jude and Lev said is true, we're going to be fine. I keep reminding myself of that. But their version of fine and my version may be very different and I still don't know why they took us. The thought makes my eyes narrow. I don't like being kept in the dark.

"Why are we here?" My grip tightens on the armrests of the freshly oiled leather wingback chair. Every inch of my body is tight with worry and something else ... something I cannot control. It's him. He's doing it to me and I hate him for it.

"I asked you a question first. Please answer it." I lift my head and square my shoulders, speaking calmly and politely, but with authority. His expressionless face gives nothing away. He sits back in his seat, letting his hand fall to the desk and taps rhythmically with his deft fingers as if he's waiting for something.

What do I know of werewolves? "Very little."

"Your tone leaves much to be desired." He slowly rises from his seat and stalks over to me. Standing directly in front of my chair, he leans against the desk as if it's a casual gesture but this close, his presence is suffocating. "That's something we need to work on, Grace." Just being this close to him is overwhelming and I shift in my seat as he crosses his arms. I love the way my name rolls off his tongue, although the fact that I love it makes me feel anxious.

I'm uncomfortable because I feel ... I feel ... I don't want to say it. Shame heats every inch of me. I shouldn't be feeling this at ease with him. I sure as hell shouldn't be fantasizing about him. Everything about this is just ... off. Once again, I question if I've been drugged. I can't look him in the eyes. I try to, but I can't bring myself to carry through with the movement.

"There's plenty we need to work on," I respond, more menacingly than I'd like.

"I have to admit that I love your smart mouth," he states as he uncrosses his powerful arms and takes my chin in his hand, forcing me to look at him. Instantly, another pulse of desire races through me. His silver eyes mesmerize me. He rubs his thumb across my bottom lip and my body betrays me by sending a hot surge of need to my core. "Although I enjoy your boldness, you aren't permitted to speak to me like that in front of the pack. Is that understood?"

I nod my head as best I can with his hand still holding my chin. Although my head is clouded and it takes me much longer than it should for me to comprehend what I've just agreed to.

"Speak, Grace." Anger courses through me at the command and I rip my head away from his grasp. I don't care if I piss him off; I refuse to let him talk to me like that.

Blinking away the haze, I reprimand him by saying, "I'm not a dog!" I raise my voice in anger and stare straight into his heated gaze. He raises his brows in surprise.

"I didn't think you were." The light in his eyes dims and he crosses his arms again, stretching the gray Henley he's wearing until it's taut, making his delectable, chiseled chest all the more visible. "When I ask you a question, I'd like you to answer me verbally." I nod my head while I stare at the desk, avoiding his scrutiny once again. I can't stand looking him in the eyes. It's as if I lose myself when I do.

After a moment of silence, I glance up at him, but not directly into his gaze. His eyes are narrowed and his lips are pressed firmly against one another, forming a hard line.

"I understand." I do my best to keep the agitation out of my voice.

"Good. Don't speak to me like that in front of the pack." His hard, absolute tone makes me feel insignificant. For some reason it also makes my heart clench in agony.

Still staring at the desk, I respond dully, "I won't."

There's movement in my periphery, but I don't bother to look at him. I need all of my energy to calm down. Now that we're in here alone, my emotions are off the damn charts. I'm exhausted and inexplicably ... sexually frustrated. I'm angry that he's talking down to me. I'm upset that I've been taken from the life I worked so hard to finally have. I feel like a shit friend for leaving Lizzie and every time I think about her, all I can see is her wounded gaze from the back seat of that car. It's all hitting me at once and it's on the verge of being unbearable.

"As far as answering your question, I'll tell you why you're here when the time is right. For now, you and Lizzie should focus on getting settled and making yourselves at home." My eyes fly to his and I part my lips to object. I want to plead with him to let us go, but he stops my appeal before it begins.

"You're a part of our pack now. There's no changing that, so you better get used to the idea of staying. The sooner, the better." I swallow my plea, but my mouth is suddenly dry. A hard lump forms in my throat, choking me. We're stuck here. They're keeping us. The tears prick again and this time I don't have the strength or energy to stop them.

I'm given a moment of reprieve when his cell phone vibrates on the desk. He doesn't speak as he answers, just holds the phone to his ear. I can't make out what the person on the other end is saying, but judging by the scowl on Devin's face, he's not exactly thrilled about the news.

"I'm sure it was a real fucking emergency." His anger lights a new sensation that flows down my arms, traveling lower until my nails dig into the leather of the chair. "I want to know as soon as his ass gets back. What about the paperwork?" He listens for a moment longer and then ends the call without another word.

Questions race through my mind.

He sets the phone on the desk and his silver eyes roam down my body before settling on my gaze again. His expression implies that he's contemplating what he should do with me. Which brings me back to my question. *Why did he take us?*

"What do you want from us?" I search his hard eyes for compassion or sympathy, but he's emotionless.

His jaw clenches. "I told you I'll tell you when the time is right." My eyes fall at his response. "Just know that you will be taken care of. You'll be safe and the pack wants nothing more than for you and Lizzie to be happy here with us." His voice softens some at the end. "It's Lizzie, right?"

I ignore his question and opt for a desperate plea over a response. "If you want us to be happy, let us go home," I beg softly to the wooden floor, unable to look him in the eye as my strength fails me.

"Enough." His hardened tone paralyzes me. "You aren't going anywhere. Get used to the idea of staying."

"I want you to come to me." I'm forced to peer into his gaze as he makes the declaration. It's hypnotizing, being caught in his heated stare. My entire body blazes.

It's too hot in here to even think.

"Come here," he commands and again his strong fingers grip my chin, traveling lower down, to my throat. I can't move. Not an inch.

My body trembles and I close my eyes, failing to gather my composure. I meet him halfway, ever so slowly, obeying.

I stiffen as his strong, muscular arms wrap around me, picking me up and pulling me into his hard chest. With only a gasp of protest, he lifts me as though I weigh nothing and settles me in his lap as he leans back in his chair. My breathing picks up and my entire body goes on high alert.

CHAPTER 6

GRACE

My head is roughly level with his chest, so Devin speaks while peering down at me. My heart thumps loudly at feeling my chest pressed tight against his. My eyes stare straight ahead at the pictures on the wall in his office. The black and white images of wooded lands are actually quite beautiful and they center me slightly. Anything to keep my mind off of him. There's something about him that's like a drug. Like heroin sinking into my veins and luring all of my senses into some depth of perversion I've never felt before.

"I'll ask you again. Please be reasonable and answer my question, Grace. What do you know about werewolves?" With a rumble in his chest, my bottom lip quivers ever so slightly. Short breaths are all I can manage.

His thumb moves in slow circles over my thigh and I find myself relaxing in his embrace. Something about him soothes me even if every bit of me is on high alert. He is the ultimate drug.

Exhaustion overwhelms me as my body eases from his touch. His hand at my hip releases me and he gently strokes up and down along the curve of my waist. I sigh at his soft touches, feeling myself slip deeper into comfort. Although he could easily run his hand up my shirt so we'd be skin to skin, he doesn't. I'm grateful for the restraint, but at the same time I crave his body against mine. For some unknown reason my anxiety seems to vanish and suddenly I can't remember what I was so concerned about. Everything just feels right and all I can think about is how good this feels. As if reading my mind, he gently pulls me into his hard chest and I allow it.

"Grace?" His voice is caressing yet still dominating.

"Yes?" I answer easily, rubbing my cheek against his chest.

"What do you know about werewolves?" he asks again, keeping his voice low and soothing. His chest rises higher with a deeper, longer inhale. I'm so relaxed that I hardly hear his words. Nuzzling into his neck, I have an intense urge to lick his throat and leave open-mouth kisses all over his chest.

As quickly as the urges come on, they leave me. *What the hell?* The realization of what I'd intended to do strikes me with a force that jolts me awake. I jerk out of his embrace and stand up so quickly I almost fall flat on my face. Devin doesn't move. He merely raises one eyebrow in question.

"Are you doing this to me?" I stare at him, meeting his gaze head-on. Of course he's doing this to me. *I'm not a damn toy he can play with!*

"Doing what?" he asks as though he has no idea.

"You know exactly what I'm talking about." I make an attempt to yell, but my cadence wavers and my voice cracks.

He stares back at me without any indication that he's even heard me. "Calm down."

Calm down? I want to cry at his response. What's happening to me? I need to get away from him. I search for the door, still disoriented and light-headed. I grip the edge of the desk to maintain my balance.

"Grace?" This time he sounds concerned and he gets up to try to steady me, but I push him away and nearly stumble into the wall, the push moving only myself and not him.

"You drugged me?" I say it as more of a statement than a question and I can't keep the sadness out of my tone. How the hell did I let that happen? I think back, searching for a moment when they could've slipped me something, but I haven't eaten anything. I haven't had so much as a single sip of water since they took us. It had to have been when I was asleep.

He approaches me cautiously, like the way one would approach a wild, wounded creature that's startled and backed into a corner. I don't blame him. I'm so unpredictable that I don't even know how I'm going to react. It's like I've lost my mind around him. He holds up his hands. "No one drugged you." He reaches for me, but I take a step back and round the desk.

"Grace, you're safe. It's okay." I shake my head at his words. The action makes me feel dizzy again. My skin feels heated and a tingling sensation takes over my limbs. He hasn't tried to grab me, but I take another step away from him to get closer to the door. My breathing is erratic and I don't know if it's from the drug or my anxiety. I try to swallow again, but I can't.

"Grace, I think you're going into shock." He stays planted where he is with his arms still raised. "Just try to calm down, okay?" I stare at him like a deer in headlights.

Shock? Is that what this is? No, that doesn't explain the urges. I bite my lip at the sordid thoughts. I've never felt this way before. My gaze travels over his body. He's absolutely gorgeous. He's got a vibe to him that lets you know he'd pin your legs back and fuck you until you begged for more and then some. My lips part and I let out a small moan as I picture it. My pussy clenches and heats.

A look of relief flashes across Devin's face almost too quickly for me to notice. I notice, though. I give him a questioning look.

"Calm down, Grace." His voice is firm now.

"No, not until you tell me what the hell is going on." I just barely get out the words while maintaining an air of authority. My body is begging me to bow to him. A hot sensation pulses through me, starting at my core and making me squirm. Something's wrong. I can't stop my facial expression from showing my desperation. My eyes plead with him to help as the tears fall.

"What did you do to me?" Any semblance of authority I had has vanished. I'm practically begging him to give me answers.

"I didn't do anything. I promise you." His eyes look so sincere, but I know something is wrong. "It's only because you're around me that you feel this way." His tone conveys his sympathy.

"Then I need to leave now!" His eyes harden and his fists clench.

"No." His stern reply offers no alternative.

My body crumples and heats, making me feel weak and light-headed once again. "I'm not okay. Please help me."

He nods his head and says, "I'll help you, sweetheart. Come here. Let me hold you." What other choice do I have? I can run, but how far would I get? I feel so weak right now. If he can help me, I'll let him. I've been told I'm independent to a fault, but I'm not stupid. My body is begging me to listen to him and obey. I cave and make my way back to him, sulking the entire time. As I near him, he sits down and opens his arms. He wants me to sit back down on his lap. I'm about to surrender to him but then I remember Lizzie, and it makes me hesitate.

"She won't be feeling what you're feeling. Not yet." His voice brings my focus back to him. I stare at his face as I try to comprehend his words.

"Why?" is all I manage to get out. He takes a deep breath, looking at the wall then back at me before he replies.

"She's not in heat yet."

"Heat?" I tilt my head in confusion. He just nods his head, maintaining eye contact. My eyes widen in shock and outrage. "Like a dog!" He grimaces and then a low growl barrels from his chest.

Chapter 7

Grace

My knees go weak as I feel an invisible force overwhelm my body, wanting me to bow to him. To lower my head to the ground and expose my neck. I drop my stare and fall to my knees, but I don't bow. I won't. The pull is so strong that it makes me feel sick to my stomach, but I refuse it, fighting it with everything in me.

"What is it with you and dogs?" He practically sneers the words. "Do you not like them?"

I shake my head, my eyes focused on his shoes.

"Speak!" I jolt at his command and a fresh stream of hot tears runs down my cheeks.

"No," I say and a shaky breath leaves me as I add, "I love

dogs." I gasp for air and finally give in, bowing to him. My cheek rests against the floor with my forearms braced on either side of my head.

He immediately lifts me up and pulls me into his chest.

"You don't need to bow to me, Grace. Not ever. Please don't." I sob against him, clinging to his powerful body as his hand cradles my head. Desperate for skin-to-skin contact, I move my hand under his shirt and up his back. I don't know why I need it, but I do.

Whatever's happening to me, I hate it. Make it stop.

"I don't mean to get angry," he says and his tone is gentle, but that doesn't take away a damn thing I currently feel. The belittling and weakness especially. I hate it all. "I don't like that you compare yourself to a dog." His free hand caresses up and down my back soothingly. He kisses my hair and I melt at his touch. I concentrate on taking deep breaths as he speaks, but at least my sobs have stopped.

"It's your cycle. You're ovulating. That's why you feel like this." I feel the rumble of his chest as he speaks and I push my body against it, loving the way the vibration feels on my skin. This is nothing like anything I've ever experienced. The need to brush my body against his is nearly intolerable. My entire being is pulsing with a desire to touch him and be touched by him.

I lick my lips and stare at his neck. There's dark stubble all the way down to his Adam's apple. I have the sudden urge to nip at his throat. I stir, trying to alleviate some of the hot ache between my legs and that's when I realize I can feel his stiffness against my thigh. He's huge. The image of him fucking me on his desk, riding me hard, comes to mind. I moan. Yes, I want him to ride me hard. I give in to the temptation and leave a hot, open-mouth kiss on his throat. My teeth pinch his skin and I pull back before letting go, knowing I'll leave a mark. Devin groans as I lean back to admire my handiwork. My chest rises and falls as I breathe heavily.

"Fuck, Grace, I'm trying to be good for you," he says as my gaze searches his face. His eyes are closed and his head is tipped back while his mouth is parted. It's so fucking sexy. I part my legs to straddle him. The move makes my hard clit throb. Resting my elbows on his shoulders, I spear my fingers through his messy hair before jerking his head to the side to bite his neck again. The move makes his dick twitch and it hits my sensitive clit. I let out a moan against his throat.

"Please." I don't even know what I'm begging for. All I know is that I need him. He can make this right.

"You want me to fuck you, Grace?" He breathes his words although they come out as a statement and not a question. I nod and faster than I can perceive, he's already moving. His fingers dig into the flesh of my hips as he lifts me up quickly, throwing my body onto the desk so that I land on my back with my legs spread wide.

"I told you to speak when I ask you a question." His tone is laced with danger as he takes a step back and backhands my clit through my jeans. *Fuck!* A fire ignites so hot in my core that my head thrashes and my limbs shake from the intensity. *Yes!*

As I come down from the overwhelming sensation, I realize he's undressing me, practically ripping my jeans off of me. With a snap and a rip, the jeans are torn halfway down my body.

Before the torn clothing even hits the floor, his tongue is on me. His rough stubble scratches against my inner thighs and it's even better than I imagined. Feeling his hot mouth on me is a dream come true. I arch my back on the desk and push myself into his face. Any sense of control is gone; I've fallen off the edge of a cliff. He growls with approval into my heat as he angles me so he can fuck me deeper with his tongue.

"Please," I beg him again. I *need* him. He continues taking his sweet time, but the sound of his zipper gives me hope. I wriggle on the desk, needing more. My body is impatient and my head thrashes from side to side. I need him now.

"Please!" I can't stand the torture any longer. I need my release. He moves from between my legs and hovers over my body while wiping my glistening arousal from his mouth with the back of his hand. His lips are swollen and his silver gaze doesn't hide his desperation to be inside me in the least. At least both of us are affected.

"You need me to fuck you, Grace?"

I don't hesitate in my answer. "Yes, I need you." As soon as the last word leaves me, his hands grab my hips and pull me to the edge of the desk while he pounds into me all the way to the hilt without a hint of mercy or shame.

"I promise it'll only hurt for a moment," he groans and I'm caught in his silver gaze. My breath is stolen, my nails digging into his forearms as he towers over me, fully inside of me. If I could speak, I'd beg him to move. It's too intense, too much.

The intense pain from being stretched begins to slowly ease as he moves inside of me.

My head drops back and I moan, the pleasure-filled waves riding up my body with every hard thrust.

"Fuck yes," he growls at the ceiling with his eyes closed and his mouth parted. He doesn't stop his steady pace, though. His head slowly drops and he opens his eyes to find mine. It's then that I notice his fangs and the hunger in his silver gaze. He is the epitome of power and lust. In this moment I am only his. I want nothing more than to bow down to him and give him every pleasure possible. My heart feels weak and raw. He has complete control of it. Sheer terror jolts through my body, freezing my hot blood. But in a flash, it's gone, leaving only the heat to scorch my sensitive skin.

My head drops to the desk and my eyes roll back from the intense pleasure radiating through my body. With one hand still on my hip and the other now wrapped around my throat, he picks up his pace and pistons into me with a primal need. I tremble as a numbness rises from the tips of my fingers and toes, threatening to overwhelm my body. I part my lips to beg for my release, but as I do he squeezes tighter around my throat and hammers into me as my pussy clenches.

"Come for me." His words are my undoing and I shatter beneath him. I *shatter* for him.

CHAPTER 8

GRACE

Devin leaves me for a moment, a chill draping itself around me as my body immediately notices his absence. I lift my head just enough to see him enter what looks to be a bathroom on the far side of the expansive office. As the aftershocks of my orgasm settle, my mind finally feels as though it's clearing. Like it's waking up from a fog. The realization of what just happened hits me with a force that makes me want to throw up.

This is why they took us.

My head shakes in denial. Shame immediately strips any sense of pleasure remaining from our bout of passion. They intend to use our bodies for their pleasure. *No.* I continue to shake my head, covering my face with my hands.

I couldn't even help myself just now. I wanted him to use me. Will I be like that around all of the other werewolves? Their very presence is a drug. It's hard to lift myself from the desk, the room spinning at the realization. Even if my body is begging for their touch, I don't want to be a whore available to them whenever they want. I want more from life. I *need* more. I push away my sadness as anger replaces it with a fierce need to rally.

Lizzie.

They will not touch her!

I push off the desk and land on my bare feet, my legs still shaking. Half-naked, I sprint to the door. The sound of my bare feet padding against the wooden floors is nothing compared to the screaming in my head. My camisole barely covers my ass, but I don't care. I need to get out of here. My limbs shake, but I run as fast as I can.

I make it to the door as Devin exits the bathroom and curses under his breath.

He's fast, but I'm at least able to grip the knob and rip the door open. I scream, "Lizzie!" Adrenaline races through my blood. There's no way I'm going to make it before he catches me. I'm going to fail her. *I already have.* As I run down the empty hall, I shout her name again. I don't make it more than a few feet before I hear the heavy thuds of men running toward me from both sides. I stumble as I realized I'm trapped and

I start to fall. My eyes dart to a door on my left, but before I can open it Devin grabs me from behind, lifting my feet off the floor and spinning me around as I scream.

"What the—" a baritone voice starts to say but Devin cuts him off as I push against his hold and squirm.

"Leave us." His hard voice echoes in the hall and footsteps scurry away in the opposite direction. His arms are wrapped around me too tightly for me to escape. But I refuse to give up, fighting and straining against him. I work one arm free and slam my elbow as hard as I can into his face.

"Fuck!"

I doubt it hurt him but it shocks him enough that he drops me and I land hard on my ass; my palms hit the ground so hard that the resulting pain makes me think I broke my wrist, but at least I didn't smack my head on the floor. I try to get to my knees at the thought of Lizzie going through what I just did. When I glance up, breathless and weighed down with worry, two silver eyes stare back at me. Lev is wide eyed at the end of the hall with his mouth agape.

Devin's hand grabs the nape of my neck as he lifts me off the floor with one arm. "I said leave!" he screams at Lev with rage vibrating off the walls. I whimper in his grasp as he wraps one arm around my waist. My hands fly up to my neck and try to pry away his fingers.

"Calm down, sweetheart." His gently spoken words against my ear are at complete odds with his powerful grip on me. But my body obeys him without my conscious consent. My hands drop to my sides as I start to see white spots dance in my vision. My body may be willing to listen to him, but my mind isn't okay with any of this. He must know that on some level because he loosens his grip but doesn't remove his hold on me. As I try to come to terms with being trapped in his arms, he tells me again that everything will be okay and that I just need to trust him.

But I don't trust him. I don't trust any of them.

Chapter 9

Devin

I leave for one fucking minute and she bolts? Rage courses through me but outwardly I'm doing my best to remain calm. Humans like controlled, collected behavior from shifters and typically I am. I have to stay composed for my mate. *My mate who doesn't even want me.*

A coldness settles inside of me, one I haven't felt in over a year. Not since I noticed her at the offering. I'll be damned if that thought doesn't hit me like a bullet to my chest. My wolf doesn't like it either. My pride is wounded. The only solace I have is that she's letting me hold her. Grace is finally settling in my arms. At least her body is. I can see in her eyes that she's resisting me. Struggling to find words to make sense of it all, I do my best to rein in my resentment that she ran right after she gave herself to me. How could she not feel our connection? How could she deny how perfect it was?

"Maybe you shouldn't have fucked her the second you got her in the house." Lev's words ring in my head. I grit my teeth to keep my irritation from showing. After all, Grace can't hear him. I don't want her to think my annoyance is with her.

"Watch it, Lev." I manage to keep a low growl from rumbling in my chest.

"I'm just looking out for my big brother. I really think it would have been better if you'd waited."

"She's in heat ... What the hell was I supposed to do? Let her suffer?"

I wait a moment for him to answer. His silence pisses me off.

"She was barely coherent." I sneer the words in my head, all the while staying relaxed on the surface for my Grace. Her body molds perfectly to mine. I've witnessed the heat before, in my old pack. I'm surprised it took me so long to realize that's what was going on with her. Especially with that sweet, intoxicating smell filling up the room. My head wasn't right with her looking at me like I was dangerous. Like I was going to hurt her. She shouldn't feel like that around me. With my touch though, she reacted like she should have.

Peering down at her small, huddled form, she presses against me with her eyes closed. She's so beautiful and serene, and now she's right where she belongs.

"How about you give her some space? The farther away she is from you, the better she'll be till the full moon."

The young wolf has a good point. I'll be able to claim her then. There wasn't a part of me that thought I'd fuck this up like I just did. *"She'll still be in pain."* The heat's a bitch. She'll writhe in agony once it hits her again.

"It won't be as bad if you stay away from her."

Grace shifts in my lap, nuzzling into my chest as her breathing evens out and deepens. Just the thought of staying away from her makes the wolf within me whine in pain.

"Easy for you to say. I've waited a year to have her. You haven't even met your mate yet. And the pull will only get stronger as the moon waxes."

I stroke her back to settle her and it seems to be helping. *"I should explain everything to her. Maybe that'll put an end to whatever's going on in her pretty little head."*

"How do you think Lizzie will react?"

I stifle a sigh. Lev makes another good point. My little brother has always been more logical than me. More empathetic, perhaps. Caleb and Dom aren't ready to tell her and Lizzie isn't in any condition to hear that news. As the Alpha of the pack, their needs come before my own. My heart hurts for my mate, though. She doesn't trust me or anything that she's feeling. For fuck's sake, she thought I drugged her.

"You could let them see each other. Caleb and Dom are going crazy because Lizzie won't come out of the bathroom and she's

crying again. Something is really wrong with her. That'll give your mate something to focus on."

"Did you get their paperwork from Vince yet?" More silence from Lev answers my question. *"He isn't back yet, is he?"* I clench my fists and scowl before I can catch myself. Thankfully, Grace has fallen asleep on my chest. The last thing I need to do is to frighten her anymore.

"Not yet."

"When he gets back, I'm going to kick his ass." Motherfucker can't listen to orders for the life of him. I know him being MIA has something to do with finding his mate, but he could've waited until things were settled here. *"What about Caleb?"*

"Haven't heard from him yet. He's probably still packing up their stuff." I nod my head even though he can't see me. The fresh scent of Grace's hair wafts toward me and I breathe her in. She smells just like she tastes, like caramel apples on a crisp autumn night. My mouth waters at the memory.

"You want some privacy, alpha?" I can hear Lev's laugh.

"Fuck off." Even as I say it, I smile. I'll get my mate's worries worked out and then everything will be perfect. It has to be. My fingers twine with her brunette locks and I bend down just enough to kiss her temple.

"Where do you want all of their shit when it gets here?"

"I want it set up exactly as it was in their place. Put it all in the east wing."

"You don't think that will freak them out?"

"They need comfort and privacy right now. They want to go home so we'll give them their home to run to."

"That's fucking crazy, Dev."

A low growl rumbles deep within my chest, causing Grace to whimper. *Fuck.* I stroke her back until she settles again.

"I'm surprised she's bothered at all by your growl. I could feel those vibes you threw at her. It knocked Jude on his ass." I can hear him chuckle.

"Yeah? It didn't get to you too?" I know it had to because it took everything in me to get her to bow. The moment she did, though, I regretted it. She's my equal. My temper will be our undoing.

"Course it did. But I stopped doing my laps and bowed like a wolf. Jude fucking dropped like a pussy." I chuckle and the movement wakes Grace. At first she's content and almost nuzzles back into me. Then her eyes open wider and she stiffens.

Damn it. This isn't how finding your mate is supposed to be.

"Well, your mate is human." My lips form a thin line at Lev's words. I run my fingers through Grace's hair and she melts back into me, although her eyes don't close.

I sigh heavily, loving the added weight of her on my chest. This would be so much better if she were a shifter. So much easier if she knew what to expect. If Grace had witnessed a heat firsthand, maybe she would've recognized it. At least her body perceives me as her mate. That's more than I can say for Dom and Caleb's mate.

CHAPTER 10

LIZZIE

Every inch of me shakes and won't stop. The nightmares come back, full force and with details that took years to forget. I'm scared to death, huddled in the corner of the shower with the curtain closed as though they don't know I'm in here. It's only an illusion and one not a piece of me believes, but it's all I have. I wonder if they know I'm not human. I pray they don't. I can't go back to what I once was.

I'm not even completely sure what I am. Latent, maybe? My old pack said I was useless and a waste. They sold me to some assholes who beat the shit out of me, trying to force my wolf to come out. Tears stream down my face and my body shakes.

They're going to hurt me. Dom looks just like *him*. Like

the shifter who brutalized my body over and over again. I shudder and squeeze my eyes shut, willing the memories to go away. I thought I'd escaped all this. I thought I was finally free. *How could this happen?* My shoulders shake uncontrollably as sobs wrack my body. I gasp for breath, but my throat dries and closes, suffocating me.

I remember the pain shooting through my back while they whipped me. Taking turns and betting on whether I would break or if the wolf would show. The small spikes piercing into my skin and gripping on before being ripped away, taking bits of bloodied flesh with it, leaving nothing but raw, broken skin and blood. Although my vision was blurred, I can still see the splatters of my blood as they hit the wall. So much blood. I can still hear their laughter as my wounds closed before their eyes, although the brutal pain remained. That's all the proof they needed. They kept at it, saying they would beat the latent out of me. That's how it works with latent wolves. They show eventually ... but mine never did.

I prayed every night for the healing to stop. I begged any and every deity who might have been listening to have mercy on me. Some nights I prayed for them to let my captors kill me. And then one night, my prayers must have been heard. I stopped being able to heal. Their confusion gave me relief, but it was short lived. They continued to torture me. They brought me to death's door over and over again. Each day they invented new ways to damage me. To bring out my wolf but she left me. Left me or died; I'm not sure which. I'm not sure if she ever even existed.

It took years before they gave up and tried to get their money back. They wanted to return me because I was broken. But my "pack" didn't recognize my scent. They denied me. I was thrown away and left in human territory for them to claim me. No one ever did. It took nearly two years of living at the shelter for the Henders to take me. They got a check for keeping me. It wasn't enough to stop them from the occasional smack and grab and push, though. Just like with everyone else, I was worthless to them. At that point I was so numb to the abuse I just accepted it as a way of life. At least they only struck me with their human fists, and I was grateful for it. They never tried to get "creative" like the shifters did.

I only started to heal when Grace took me in.

"Grace." I sob her name into the cold tile wall. *Please come help me.* I can't even speak the words aloud since my throat hurts too much. *Come hold me.* I wrap my arms around my shoulders and rock back and forth. She's the only one who's ever cared about me. I squeeze tighter as my head falls and rests on my knees. The only one who's ever touched me in a kind way. I won't survive here. I know it. This will kill me. With my last bit of energy, I whisper, "Please save me."

PART III
THE BETAS

CHAPTER 11

DOM

The sound of my mate crying is killing me. My chest feels hollow as I lean my forehead against the door to her temporary room. Her sobs never stop and my touch is useless to console her. I don't understand; it's not supposed to be like this. Her whispers echo in my head and my wolf whines in absolute torment. Rage replaces the agony ... toward my wolf and myself. I should be able to soothe her, to be a balm to her broken soul. Instead, I'm the one causing her pain. The way she looks at me with sheer terror in her eyes shatters any hope I have at claiming my mate.

I need to do something, but how can I help her when she won't let me anywhere near her? I don't know what the hell to do. I pound my fist against the wall in fury. My only consolation is that our Alpha's mate can calm her to the point that she's still. I'll do anything to heal Lizzie, to have her whole and happy. But first she needs to let me the hell in. The sooner, the better.

A scowl mars my face as Caleb approaches the door. I don't want to share her. Fate's a real bitch.

"She's not letting you in?" His voice is low, with more than a hint of worry.

"No shit." I practically spit out the words but he doesn't flinch at my tone. He's already used to my bitterness over this situation.

"We should tell her we're her mates."

I just barely resist the urge to knock him out. I'm worried about healing our mate and he's worried about fucking her. I grit my teeth but manage a response. "Do you see the way she looks at me?" I say. He ignores my words like the stubborn asshole he is.

"Let's just do it," he says and I shake my head. "It'll be like ripping off a bandage."

"I can feel the hate and fear radiating off of her all the way from here and you expect me to tell her she's my mate."

"*Our* mate!" I can't look at him so I just stare at the wall. "If we don't, then what's going to happen when her heat hits? What about three days from now when the full moon comes and we have to claim her?" He's out of his fucking mind.

"Have to claim her? We don't *have* to claim her."

"You don't want her?" Shock and disbelief are both present in his voice, but also overwhelming sadness. "How can you not want our mate?"

"Of course I want our mate!" His audible exhale is heavy with relief even though my words came out as a low growl. Caleb is truly out of his fucking mind if he thinks she'll roll over and let us claim her. Her terror is so thick it drenches the air around me. My next words come out easy. "We can wait till the next full moon. Or however long it takes."

"I'm not waiting. And I'm not risking her heat coming on and it fucking us over like it fucked over Alpha."

I finally meet his gaze, which stops him from pacing the hall. "How is he?" I heard him and Lev earlier but tuned them out to give my mate all my attention. Lizzie had been saying something in between sobs but all I could understand was *Grace*. It's clear she loves her Alpha and it breaks my heart that she has so much love for her, but only hate and fear for me.

"Not looking too good. She ran from him."

"What the fuck?" My brow rises with shock. None of this is happening the way it should.

"Yeah, when he caught up to her, she knocked him in the jaw trying to get away."

Holy shit. The admiration in Caleb's voice is comical, complete with a cocky grin although the humor doesn't reach his eyes. No one's gotten a hit on the Alpha in years.

Of course his own mate, a *human* mate, would get the best of him. It almost makes me smile. Almost. But I don't. So both of our mates have a bit of a violent streak? I can't help the fact that the Alpha's mate hitting him makes me feel a little better about my own mate.

"But she reacts to him." I saw her melt into him at the offering. Despite being petrified for Lizzie, she was perfectly fine in his embrace. "And that's the way it should be." Now I'm the one pacing as Caleb leans against the wall.

He comments, "Yeah and then her heat hit and it freaked her out."

"Why?" I don't understand how wanting her mate's touch could possibly hurt their relationship.

"According to Lev, abducting them, not telling them why, and then fucking them is not a good idea. Judging by how pissed off Devin is, I'm going to have to agree."

A grimace spreads across my face as I say, "You make it sound way worse than it is."

He raises his brows and says, "Not really. Anyway, she rejected him after they bonded."

Oh shit. I'm sure Devin's hurting after that. "But she's his mate."

"He hasn't told her yet and that's why I want to tell Liz."

"It's Lizzie." I narrow my eyes as jealousy creeps up on me. Shit, I don't even like him saying her name. There's no fucking way we're going to be able to share her.

"First of all, we need to tell her so he can tell Grace. He won't tell her because he wants to make sure Liz will be all right first. He's waiting for us to be ready. I know he's sacrificed for the pack before, but we're also hurting his mate. She's our new Alpha." He stresses the last bit and I feel my resolve crumble.

It kills me to admit it but I don't have any other ideas on how to get through to Lizzie. Maybe telling her will help; she can't get any worse.

"And second," he continues and Caleb's authoritative voice brings my concentration back to him. "Stop thinking like that. I hate that you're all pouty that we're sharing our mate." My brows knit together in anger.

"Get out of my head, Caleb."

"You know I can't." At least he has the decency to sound remorseful. "We'll make it work. Fate fucked us over for a reason, right?" He reaches out and pats me on the back, his black boot kicking off of the wall as he does. "Maybe we're both too messed up for her on our own," he adds and grins wickedly before continuing, "but together we'll be whole for her." I snort. *Real romantic.*

"The only problem with that theory is that we're the same kind of messed up."

He lets out a low chuckle. "No way, you're way more fucked up than I am." He smiles broadly at me and for the first time since I realized that we were going to have to share

Lizzie, I don't resent him. "It wouldn't kill you to smile, you know?" And just like that, the urge to knock him out comes back. I shove him into the wall.

"I'm just screwing around." I know he is, but it really might make a difference for Lizzie if I could lighten up some. *Scary as hell* seems to be the most common description of me from the humans. I decide to change the subject. "Vince back yet?"

"Not that I've heard." I watch as Caleb's fists clench. He usually doesn't get his feathers all ruffled. Out of all of us, he's the lighthearted smooth talker. Vince is in for a world of hurt when he gets back. Nearly everyone in the pack is pissed at him. He was supposed to have Lizzie's background info ready for us. We already had Grace's since Devin practically stalked her this past year, but we didn't know Lizzie was ours until yesterday.

Instead, he hightailed it out of the offering and hasn't been back since. He felt his mate in the audience but he's going to have to wait until she's offered, just like Devin had to. He can't just take her. I have to believe he isn't that stupid. It's been nearly twelve hours since we last touched base with him, though. That's entirely too long for him to not be up to something that's going to fuck us over. He can't be hanging around in human territory; he knows better than that. I shove down my thoughts before they get the best of me.

"So you got all of their stuff in there?"

"Yeah, it's time to move them into their new home."

"It's weird."

He shrugs at my comment. "It's what Alpha wanted and I think it'll help them adjust."

Devin wanted the rooms set up exactly like their apartment. They have the entire east wing all to themselves. It has everything but a kitchen. Plus now they'll each have their own bedroom and bathroom instead of sharing like they were before. Although, given their dependency, I'm not sure they'll sleep apart for a while.

My wolf whines again, hating that fact.

"Honestly, it's not a bad idea. It'll give them a sense of home and safety." His words hit me hard and I scowl. "I know, man." He pats my back again, a firmer, harder pat that pisses me off but when he smirks, I smack him away. At least I know he's feeling the same way. "One day we'll be her home and safety." He nods his head as if he's reassuring himself. I can only hope he's right.

CHAPTER 12

GRACE

I wake up in Devin's arms. The Alpha. I breathe out deeply and snuggle into his warm hold, nuzzling into his hard chest. I sigh and feel my cheeks heat as I remember him taking me, shattering me. And then my eyes widen. I sit straight up. Something's wrong. I shouldn't be cuddled up to him as if he's the oxygen I breathe.

My heat.

That's what's wrong with me. I begged him, literally begged him, to fuck me. The shame and guilt washing over me make my heart clench and I have to close my eyes. My fingers go numb and my stomach sinks. *I can't do this. Where's Lizzie?*

"Calm down, sweetheart." Devin's words are accompanied

by his arms around me, holding me there in his lap and I wish I could simply push him away. He traps me gently, but still it's against my will. He runs his fingers through my hair and pulls me back into his chest. I resist slightly but I want to lie against him. My body's pulled to him and I can't help it. It's as though my body and mind are two separate entities; I don't like the loss of control. It's disturbing.

He strokes my back and I feel myself relax into him. This power he has over me does nothing to ease my racing thoughts. A part of me thinks I should leave it be and give in. It isn't like I have a choice. But that's just not how I was made. He commanded me, fucked me, and now he's petting me like a prized poodle. I'm not going to sit back and be a good little pack-bitch.

"Why did you take us?" The words come out dead on my tongue. I already know the answer, but I need to hear him say it. Maybe then I can hate him. I can stop feeling this intense emotional and physical pull to him. His hand pauses as his back tenses for a split second, his strong muscles rippling.

"I wish you would trust your instincts." His comment is followed by a low and irritated sigh. Gritting my teeth, I shift in his lap so I'm facing him and stare up at his gorgeous face, ready to lay into him, to push him away and practically spit out every horrible thought I have. His silver eyes look almost sad. They soften my resolve to be combative. He rests his hands on my hips and says, "I wish you would trust me, Grace.

I know you want to."

My mind is at war with itself to the point that I have to look away. He's right. I do have the desire to trust him, to let him hold me, to give myself to him. But that's not who I am. "Because of my heat." I frown and offer the words as a simple explanation. Once the heat is gone, I'm sure I won't feel this way about him anymore. It's only temporary. But I'll live with this forever ... and Lizzie ...

Devin's fingertips dig into the soft flesh at my hips. The possessive hold makes my body instinctively still. My heart races in fear. Once he registers my reaction, he loosens his grip and caresses instead, but I remain frozen in place as my heart tries to climb up my throat. I want to trust him, but I sure as fuck don't.

A moment of awkward silence passes.

"How long did I sleep?" I ask and peek up at him through my lashes only to find him staring at me. As though he's studying me.

"A few hours." Shock widens my eyes and I jump back a bit, as far as I can with his hands still gripping my hips, keeping me seated in his lap.

"Lizzie," I say her name in a breathy voice, not hiding my fear and shock. I can't believe I left her alone for that long.

"She's all right." I shift uncomfortably in my captor's grasp. Would he tell me if she wasn't? As if on cue, he speaks up.

"I'd let you know if she wasn't well. She seems to like her

space and we're giving it to her."

I nod my head, but eye him questioningly. I almost ask him, promise? As if this man owes me anything or that I should trust him. But I don't have to ask. He tells me exactly what I want to hear.

"I promise nothing bad will happen to her. She's sleeping. Sound asleep and perfectly safe."

"She's not with—"

"She's not with a man, no. No one has ... touched her. Like I've touched you." There's a thrumming in my veins and mixed feelings that race through me.

Before I can whisper *promise?* yet again, he says it first. "I promise you, Grace."

Jude said they can hear each other's thoughts and now I'm wondering if he can hear mine. I purse my lips and narrow my eyes.

"What's wrong?" He seems a bit worried so I school my expression back to neutral. Still, I can't help but to ask.

"Can you read my mind?" At my question he chuckles, revealing his perfect, yet deadly white teeth. I find myself staring at his sharp fangs, mesmerized by them.

"No, I can't read your mind. Werewolves can communicate telepathically if we concentrate but that doesn't include humans." He runs his fingers through my hair and his silver eyes sparkle almost as brilliantly as his smile. "So unfortunately I'll never be able to read your mind, Grace."

His fingertips glide gently up and down my back, pulling at my cream camisole. It's then that I realize I'm only wearing my shirt. He's covered my lower half with a cashmere throw. I snuggle into it and shift my weight on his lap, feeling self-conscious. My eyes search the room and land on my ripped jeans and lace thong. Dammit. I can't help but frown at the sight.

"Those were my favorite jeans. I just got them." I can't conceal the disappointment in my voice. His eyes follow my gaze and he runs a hand through his gorgeous hair, looking guilty all the while.

"We'll get you more. The clothes from your apartment are here so you have plenty of outfits to choose from in the meantime. The betas are setting up your room." I perk up immediately.

"Our things are here?" I blink rapidly at him as my mind wakes up.

He smirks at my excitement and nods. I instantly glare at him. He'd better speak when I ask him a question. This shit's going to work both ways.

His eyes spark at the sight of my narrowed eyes. "Yes," he says teasingly.

"I swear to God, if you can read my mind, I'm going to beat the shit out of you." An asymmetric grin pulls at his lips.

"I told you I can't. I won't ever lie to you, Grace." The whimper that leaves me at the sound of his tender tone is ... unexpected. As is the desire to lean in closer.

It's hitting me again ... squirming in his lap, I close my eyes to will it away.

"I asked you one question and you still haven't answered it." The words rumble from his chest as I lean into him even more. I nuzzle under his chin and resist the need to nip at him. The temptation is nearly overwhelming and just the thought fans the low flames igniting my core.

"And what was that question again?" I really don't remember. I'm still tired and this day feels like one giant blur of raw emotion.

"What do you know about werewolves?" He leans back in his chair and I lean back too. A little distance is good.

Oh, right. I swallow and pick at the ends of the throw as I shrug against him. "Not much, really."

"And what is 'not much?'"

"Well, I know you shift into a very large wolf. You're good at smelling and hearing. You hate vampires." I bite the inside of my cheek and try to think of more. "I *now* know that you all have silver eyes and you're taller than average." I push the throw down and lean back into him. Staring at the black and white photographs on the far office wall I comment, "You have the ability to make unsuspecting women sleep with you."

A low growl rumbles up his chest as a warning.

"That's pretty much it."

"You're right; that isn't very much at all. And half of it's wrong." I scrunch up my nose and feel my forehead crease.

pull away from him, both my palms pressing against his chest as I stare into his piercing silver eyes.

"What did I get wrong?"

"We're not all *taller than average*." He mocks me. "I don't like what you said about making women sleep with us." I'm forced to bite my tongue at that comment, so much so I'm surprised I don't bleed. "We don't all have silver eyes. And lastly, we don't hate vampires."

"Yes you do." The words come out accusingly. "That's why we have the treaty. You keep them away."

A slight frown mars his handsome face at my words, but he nods. "They stay away because we asked. But that doesn't mean that we hate them."

"You just asked them to stay away?"

"Well no, not exactly. We have an understanding." I raise my brows, willing him to continue. "They stay away or we kill them."

"But you don't hate them?"

He shakes his head. "Why is that so hard to believe?"

"I was always told you came to Shadow Falls to hunt them because they're your natural enemies."

He scoffs. "Not at all. A mate to one of the pack members was in danger. We had to protect her."

"A mate?"

"Yes," he says and his response is clipped.

"Whose mate?"

"The grandfather to the Alpha of my old pack."

"I don't understand. This is the same pack, isn't it? There's only one pack who we made the treaty with."

"We're part of that pack. I fought their Alpha for the territory after forming my own pack." The curious side of me itches to scoot closer to him. I need to know more.

"Tell me everything from the beginning," I say then cross my legs in his lap and watch him intently.

His grin in response is contagious. "I will, sweetheart." He shakes his head and adds, "Not today, though. It has to be two or three in the morning." My gaze wanders around the room, searching for the source of the ever-present soft ticking. Damn, he's right. The simple, sleek and modern clock on the wall directly behind me reads nearly 2:30 a.m.

"I'm happy you seem more relaxed now." His words are soothing as I hum a response into his chest. He smells so fucking good. Like a masculine, woodsy pine.

"You're like a drug." The words slip past my lips effortlessly. "It's not right and I don't like it."

He leans down and runs his teeth along the shell of my ear, causing a chill to run through me while his hot breath tickles my skin. He whispers, "I love that I'm your drug."

The shiver morphs into a spike of need and I rub myself against him, just barely containing my moan.

"Grace." His tone holds a note of warning.

"Yes?" My response is practically a purr and I don't recognize this person. With a desperate need riding over me, I lean forward just to smell him, just to get a small dose of that lust. The tip of my nose runs along his stubble and a warmth flows through me. It's like ... like fate telling me everything is going to be all right. "I've never felt like this before," I confess to him.

"Grace," he warns me, but even his authoritative tone is weakened like I am. He feels it too. I steady myself against him, rocking slightly.

With his hands on my hips, he stops my movements. I murmur, "But I need you."

"Fuck," he groans to the ceiling as his head rolls back at my words.

"Please, fuck me." I have no shame this time. I'm throbbing against him with desire and I have no intention of being denied. My nipples are pebbled and all I can think about is him inside of me, thrusting and soothing every need I have. I splay my hand against his chest and push. With little resistance, he leans back into the chair, his hooded eyes finding mine.

With my chest pressed against him, I place my lips at his ear. "I want you. And you better not fucking deny me." He groans and takes my head in his hands as his lips crash against mine. His warm tongue runs along the seam of my lips and my mouth parts for him. My tongue dances with his as he struggles to release his hard dick from his pants. His movements beneath me make it obvious that he's stroking himself and that knowledge makes my skin heat even more with anticipation as I moan. I need him inside of me, filling me.

I position myself so that the head of his dick is at my hot entrance. He stares into my eyes as I gently glide down his massive cock. My bottom lip drops and I can barely hold his gaze. A strangled moan is torn from me as I move down his length, taking every inch of him. I'm still a little sore from earlier, but the fullness makes my body sing with pleasure. I move back and forth a few inches, whimpering as my limbs tremble slightly. My head falls onto his shoulder as the hot sensation overwhelms me. Devin takes my head in his hands and kisses me sweetly. I moan into his mouth as I glide up and down, my arousal making the movement effortless although his girth is still stretching me. I lean back and pick up my speed while my hands rest on his muscular pecs, riding him at my own pace.

He's good to me, I tell myself. Some part of me that sees this pathetic need as weak. I choose who I want to fuck and when. This is me, taking what I want. I won't be ashamed of that.

His hands stay at my hips as he takes my nipple into his warm mouth, bites down and pulls back. I arch my back at the spike of pleasure and wanton heat in my core. He relaxes against the chair, watching me with a hungered look in his silver eyes. Everything about him screams power and need. *He needs me.* The thought is heady.

His heated gaze of adoration sends yet another surge

of arousal through me. My clit hits his pelvis with every downward stroke as I continue riding him and it makes my pleasure all the more intense.

I stop my movements and stare at him. He's letting me ride him. He's given me control. But it's false control. I find myself wanting him to fight for it. A moment passes before Devin looks up at me. He bucks his hips against me, causing me to moan as his eyes find mine. As we both catch our breath he asks, "What's wrong, sweetheart?"

I pause for a moment before admitting the truth. "I want you to fight me, to take me."

Before I can blink, he's lifted us out of the chair and he spins my body around, pinning me against the wall. It's cool against my flesh. I don't even have time to gasp until my cheek is pressed against the wall with his fist gripping my hair. My legs are spread wide and just the head of his hard dick is nestled between my folds. Both my wrists are captured in one of his hands and held above my head. *Holy fuck!* My heart races in my chest. His speed and strength are terrifying but somehow invigorating at the same time. His other hand loosens its grip in my hair, then slips between the wall and my body, moving lower and lower until he's able to circle my clit with heavy, unrelenting pressure. The feeling is so intense that I try to move away, but I'm trapped. I can hardly move any part of my body.

He whispers into my ear, "You questioning my dominance,

sweetheart? My pussy clenches at his words, feeling empty without him inside me. I shake my head slightly as best I can. "No," I murmur, my eyes barely open as the pleasure rocks through me.

Without warning, he slams his dick inside of me all the way to the hilt and I scream out his name while an orgasm rips through my body. He groans into my neck, "I know you love me destroying your cunt, you're so fucking tight on my dick."

His words bring me that much closer to yet another release as he starts rutting me from behind. I love every bit of what he's doing to me. I can hardly take it, but at the same time I want more. I want all of him. I need all of him. My heart clenches in agony as I find myself wanting to beg, but I don't know what for. His lips kiss over my shoulder and neck hungrily. I feel his fangs skim across my neck and I push myself into them. *Yes!*

He nips my ear and sucks on my neck, quickening his pace.

The sound of his hips slamming into me fuels my need to let go. I try to move away as the feeling becomes too much. I try everything to escape, but I'm pinned. I can't get away from the intensity of the need running through my body, heating and numbing every inch of me.

"I don't think so, sweetheart. You wanted me to fuck you like this, remember?" The danger in his voice is intoxicating. I was a fool to think I could fight him. "Take it, sweetheart." His low growl sends even more desire strumming through me and just as I'm about to find my release all over again, he pinches my clit, making me scream. My orgasm hits me like the rough waves of the ocean, crashing unforgivingly against the shore over and over as my body trembles uncontrollably. At the same time, I feel him release, heightening my own pleasure as his dick throbs inside of me.

"Tell me you felt that, sweetheart. Tell me you feel our connection." He breathes heavily into my neck and his words come out with desperation. I've had sex before. Plenty of times. But this is ... it's more. He adds, "I'm not letting you go till you do."

Our connection. It's far too much. The violent crash is imminent and it's going to destroy me. Not even a day, and I already know Devin is going to ruin me. It's not fair. I never stood a chance.

I can't lie. "Yes." I answer him as quickly as I can and I feel his body relax against mine, but he still cradles me against him. I catch my breath and say, "I promise I felt it." Thankfully I stop myself before the next words slip out. My heart clenches and tears form in my eyes when I realize how close I was to blurting out three stupid words that should never be spoken.

CHAPTER 13

DOM

Caleb takes a deep breath in front of her bathroom door before glancing over his shoulder at me and asking, "You ready, man?"

Clearing my throat, I deny my own uncertainty. Honestly, I don't know if I am. My wolf hurts being away from her, but it's bearable compared to the pain I felt when she rejected me. The east wing is finished, every piece in its place, so we figured we'd get our little mate settled.

She wasn't in the guest bedroom. Not that I expected her to be in bed waiting for us; I'm not that naïve.

"She probably fell asleep in there." I nod at Caleb's assertion as he gestures to the bathroom.

It kills me that she's avoiding us, but I'm not going to lie down and just take this shit forever. She's my mate, and I'll be damned if she's going to refuse me without giving me a chance.

"Come on, stop dragging your feet. She's probably asleep anyway." He reaches for the bathroom door before I'm even able to respond. It's locked. That's not surprising. He jiggles the handle and it pisses me off. He's being too loud. He's going to wake her up and I'd rather he didn't. If she's asleep I can at least hold her without having her attack me. That thought, that possibility, is the only thing that drives me to do this right now. Rather than just leave her be in peace until she's ready to come out. I grit my teeth and push him out of the way.

"Knock it off. I swear to God if you woke her up, I'm going to break your hand." He snorts and all out smiles at my threat.

"You may be a big motherfucker, but I can still take you, Dom." The idea of the two of us going at it puts a wicked grin on my face. Not many in the pack like to spar with me anymore. I take a credit card out of my wallet and slip it between the lock and the doorframe. I'm not as good as some, but I'm sure I can jimmy this lock.

"Put your money where your mouth is, pup."

"Pup? I'm six months younger than you." I chuckle at the indignation in his tone that rings in my head.

"Still younger." As I whisper the words, I hear the lock clear and I twist the knob. We're in. Holding my breath, I push the door open as quietly as possible. I silently step into the room, but she's not here. My brows furrow and Caleb pushes past me. I take another glance around the large bathroom, but she's nowhere to be seen. Adrenaline spikes through me and my heart beats frantically, pounding against my rib cage. My throat closes and I struggle to take in a breath.

As I'm having a goddamn breakdown, Caleb pulls open the shower curtain. The sound of the rings sliding along the metal bar steals my attention.

"Calm down; she's right here." I release a breath I didn't know I was holding and walk silently, but quickly to my mate.

She's curled up on the bottom of the deep soaking tub, lying awkwardly against the cold cast iron so that her neck is at a weird angle. That's got to fucking hurt. She could've at least grabbed a towel for a makeshift pillow. That now familiar pain creeps up in my chest. She'd rather stay hidden and cold than to attempt any kind of comfort. Shit, we left her alone in the bedroom; she could've slept there. I breathe in deep, letting the disappointment and guilt run through my body. She doesn't trust us.

I lean down to sit on the edge of the tub and brush her soft blond hair away from her face. Her cheeks are tearstained and black mascara is smeared under her eyes, but she's still impossibly stunning. Her petite frame only takes up about half of the tub, making her look even more fragile. Her deep, even breathing confirms that she's out cold. She's still in her skimpy dress; I can't help it as my eyes linger on her upper half that's very much in danger of being exposed. The bottom of her dress doesn't even come close to covering her ass. I tilt my head and I can see a bit of a cream-colored lace thong. I close my eyes and bite back a groan. She's fucking gorgeous. I sure as hell don't deserve her.

I consider undressing her and putting her in something more comfortable but nix that idea as soon as it pops into my fucked-up brain. She doesn't even want me to hold her hand. There's no way she'll be all right if I undress her.

Caleb picks up her heels on the other side of the tub and looks them over. "It's a wonder she hasn't broken her damn neck wearing these things." I snort. Her toenails are painted hot pink and match her dress perfectly.

"You think pink's her favorite color?" I don't know why I ask. The thought slips out.

"Judging by all the pink shit we just brought here, yeah." I nod my head, idly wondering what else she likes. I want to know everything about her. My eyes drift down her luscious curves.

"I grabbed this to cover her up," Caleb says. I turn around to face Caleb although I have to look up at him since I'm still seated on the edge of the tub. He's holding the comforter from the bed she could've easily slept in. I nod and exhale deeply while I stand. I didn't even realize he'd left the room.

"All right, let's wrap her in it so we can get her to her room." I move out of his way. *"You think Alpha's going to have Grace sleep with him tonight?"* I'm still debating on sleeping next to

Lizzie. I'll wake up before her, so I can slip out before she has a chance to freak out. He huffs, giving me a look like I should know better.

"*I think he'd like to, but he's not going to have much of a choice.*" I tilt my head and give him a side-eye. He just shakes his head and reaches down to collect our mate. "*You really think Grace is going to want to sleep with him tonight?*" I frown and shrug. I don't understand why our mates are so difficult.

Caleb stands in the tub, draping the comforter over her body. I bend down with him to help gather the blanket around her tiny body. As I tuck the blanket under her arm, her blue eyes spring open and stare straight into mine, scaring the shit out of me. I stumble back a bit, caught off guard. My action halts Caleb and he follows my gaze to our mate's eyes. I hear her heartbeat pick up, instantly racing, but outwardly she shows no signs that she's coherent. Her body is frozen in place and her face is devoid of emotion. She reminds me of an animal playing dead, hoping a predator will go away and leave her alone.

I raise my hands to show her that I don't mean her any harm. "You all right, little one?" I keep my voice as reassuring as I can, trying to calm her. She doesn't answer. Her eyes dart to my hands then back to my face. The sound of her heart beating chaotically fills the small room it's so damn loud, but she remains rigid and tense. Something about her expression has changed, though. She's no longer a wounded animal; the hint of silver in her eyes sparks in a way that makes me aware she's waiting to strike. She wants to fight me. As much as that thought makes my dick hard, this isn't her challenging my worthiness as a mate. I wish that were the case. I'd pin her ass down so fast and fuck her ruthlessly till she had no doubt who she belonged to. But that's not what this is. The smell of fear, not arousal, permeating the air is so strong it's practically suffocating.

"Liz, you fell asleep in the tub, baby; we were just going to move you so you would be more comfortable." Caleb slowly steps out of the tub as he talks to her, but Liz's eyes don't leave mine. She shows no sign that she's heard him. I part my lips to say something, but I don't know what the hell to say. She's obviously scared out of her mind. She's looking at me like I'm her worst enemy. What the hell did I do to put her on edge?

"Lizzie, you okay?" Still no response. If I could just touch her, then I could calm her down. I know I could. I could make her *feel* this connection, this electric pull between us. My thoughts give me the push I need to move toward her. Swallowing thickly, I slowly reach down with the intention of stroking her arm, but she silently rears back and scrambles to get away from me. I pull back and put my hands up again, showing her that I won't reach out to her. The comforter restricts her movement as she struggles to get up. Her feet slip, caught up in the blanket and I'm too damn slow to stop her from bashing the back of her head against the spout.

She winces as both of her hands shoot up to cradle the wound on her head. The distinct smell of blood reaches me instantly. I reach down for her again, wanting to help her, *needing* to help her. I know that had to hurt. But as my large hand palms her chin she screams, kicking furiously against the comforter as her nails dig into my forearm and her teeth sink into the flesh of my hand.

"Fuck!" I pull back before her teeth release me, spilling more blood than necessary. Blood seeps from the two large scratches she left on my arm. I stare at them in surprise before turning my eyes back to her. My blood glistens on her lips and her sharp blue eyes stare back at me full of hate. My gut drops and I swallow the lump forming in my throat, which feels too tight to breathe. I can only hope that the look on my face conveys how torn up I am.

"Hey now, baby girl, you're all right." Caleb moves in front of me to catch Lizzie's eye. She ignores him, continuing to stare at me with utter hatred. "Dom's just trying to help you, baby." He kneels on the tub without reaching for her. "It's okay. I promise we aren't going to hurt you."

Her small voice hisses her words dripping with venom. "Don't let him touch me."

At her statement, I feel my soul shatter into jagged pieces as my wolf howls in agony. And then I hear something I shouldn't. It takes me a moment in my despair to realize that it came from my mate. Caleb looks at me with disbelief, giving me confirmation that he heard it as well. I stare into those icy blue eyes and will her to speak again. She doesn't, though. Her wolf is silent. But I know I heard her whine in pain.

Our mate's a werewolf.

I scent the air, but I can't smell her wolf at all. If Caleb hadn't heard her also, I would be doubting my sanity.

I push Caleb to the side to stand in front of our mate. He doesn't resist at all. He's looking at her with a look of pure confusion. "Where'd your wolf go?"

A look of dread crosses her face. I see her swallow as she pushes her body as far away from us as the tub will allow. All traces of anger have dispersed, leaving only fear.

Staggered breaths leave her parted lips, and tears well in her eyes.

"Why are you so scared, little one?" I hold up my arm for her to see. "It's okay. I'm not mad." Her shoulders start rising and falling as her breathing becomes erratic.

"It's okay," Caleb finally speaks up. "What happened to your wolf?" She shakes her head violently. Why is she so terrified of us? More importantly, how the hell is she hiding her wolf like that?

"I'm not a werewolf." The rushed words barely have any sound as they leave her lips.

My eyes narrow at her. "Don't lie to me, little one." I try to keep the threat out of my voice, but it's still there. The moment I hear the admonishment, I regret it. She's fucking terrified. I shouldn't be giving her more reasons to fear me.

"She left me," our scared little mate whimpers. "I'm not latent anymore, she won't come back." She gasps for breath as her body shakes. "Please, she won't come back." I feel my heart hollow as my wolf whines in distress.

"Please what, little one?"

"Please don't beat me." Her sad blue eyes burrow into mine as she begs, "Please don't hurt me again. I swear she won't come. She's dead. I can't shift. I swear I can't shift." Her words are barely coherent, but I've heard enough that I understand her terror. I close my anguished eyes. Now I get why she hates me and it shreds my insides.

If I could bring my father back to life, I would.

When I killed him, it was for me but if I could do it again, I'd torture him first for her.

"It wasn't me." I choke the pitiful words out. I was just a child, just a pup, but I knew what my family was doing. I knew what my father did to those kids, but it took years for me to gather the courage to fight him. Years of listening to their tormented screams. He recorded everything as proof of their identity when he sold them on the black market. As I grew older, he made me watch. First the videos and then in person. I'll never forget their haunted eyes as my father and uncles beat them mercilessly, forcing their animals to the surface. His large hand on my shoulder kept me pinned in place as he made me watch. Even as I vomited in revulsion, he insisted I needed to see it to be a man.

The day he handed me a weapon to do as he told me, as my Alpha commanded, was the day I fought back. I bludgeoned him with the bat he used to break his victims' bones. By the end of our battle, we'd both shifted and he lay in front of me coughing up blood with what little life he still had left. Before he could heal, I ripped out his throat; his hot, sticky blood gushed into my mouth before spilling onto the floor. The only regret I've ever had in my entire life was not stopping him sooner. If I hadn't been so scared of dying, I could've saved nearly half a dozen children. I never once had any remorse over killing him. Not until today. I wish he were still alive so I could kill him for her. So she could watch as her tormentor took his last breath.

"It wasn't me. It was my father."

"Just stay away," she cries and I swear my heart breaks.

"It wasn't me," is all I can answer, the words only a whisper.

Caleb's consoling hand on my shoulder brings me back to the present. Back to my sobbing, shattered mate. She's so fucking damaged. My heart aches for her. I reach out my hand to her unable to stop myself, but she backs herself into the corner like a scared animal. Her rejection is deserved as I drop my head in shame. I take a deep breath and square my shoulders.

Now that I know why she's been acting the way she has, I can make this right. I'll fix this.

I meet Caleb's eyes. "Bring her to the bedroom."

PART IV
THEIR MATES

CHAPTER 14

DOM

"**W**hat the hell, Dom?" Even though he's screaming in my head, Caleb looks back at me with a neutral expression.

"She's scared. I'm going to fix it."

"By tying her up?" His shocked tone is laced with disapproval. *"She's scared out of her mind, you sick asshole!"*

"Knock it the fuck off," I sneer with disdain before calming myself and adding, *"you know I'm not going to cross the line."* He presses his lips into a thin line, his hands clenching into fists before quickly relaxing and then he looks back at our mate. She's still huddled in a ball shaking uncontrollably, intently focused on ignoring us. As though we don't exist if she can't see us. She's got the blanket cocooned around her

ke it's going to protect her. I shake my head at the sight of her. *Nothing's coming in between us, little one.*

"*Tying her up is crossing the line.*" His low growl is fortified with an unspoken threat.

"*Bring it on, motherfucker.*" The low growl I thought was inaudible awards me with a small whimper from our mate. One that shreds me. "*I'm doing this for her.*" I leave him with anger pouring off of him in waves. With long, determined strides, I make my way to the other side of the estate. I need to gather rope from the dungeon. I couldn't care less if Caleb doesn't like it. She may be both of ours, but that isn't going to stop me from doing right by her on my own. She needs to be subdued and reconditioned. Now that I know what she's been through, all bets are off. Our mate isn't a scared little human afraid of the big bad werewolves. No, she's an abused, latent wolf in desperate need of being given a kind, devoted touch. Except she's shown she'll fight us tooth and nail before she lets that happen. She'll do anything to keep us away because she's petrified. All of her past experiences have her on edge and frightened.

I scowl thinking of what she's been through. My chest tightens and my throat constricts. My poor mate. Fate's one cruel bitch. She's scared of me and by extension all of us, simply because I look just like my father. Just like the man who bought her and tortured her. She's been taught to fear the very sight of me. I know just as well as her what he's done and seen how his victims look at him with sheer terror in their eyes. That's how she looks at me. I clench my fists and grip on to the rage and resentment; better that than the sadness threatening to destroy the last bit of hope I have of claiming my mate.

She may have learned to fear my presence, but I can retrain her. I'll have to tie her down at first so she can't hide from me. That way she won't be able to ignore me or run from me anymore. I nod my head as I collect what I'll need. I'll soothe her and relieve her of her agony. Instead of the pain and fear she's used to, I'll condition her mind to crave my touch and her body to want me. She'll let go of the past once she can see her future with me.

Then there's the issue of her latency. Her wolf was there. I heard the poor broken creature whimper in pain; she reached out to our wolves. But somehow Lizzie held her back and hid her. She vanished; there one split second and gone the next. We couldn't hear her or feel her or even scent her. It doesn't make any sense. I should know, since latent shifters were my father's main perversion. You can't hide your wolf. They're always able to be heard, felt and eventually seen. Even if you're latent and can't shift, there's always something that will bring your animal to the surface. Lizzie, my sweet, haunted mate, is not *latent*. She's something else and I have no fucking clue what. But her wolf is in there somewhere and my own wolf is chomping at the bit to get to her. He knows she's hurting and he claws at me to protect her.

If only it were that easy. If only you could protect

someone from their past.

My strides pick up as I get closer to my mate. I've only been gone a few minutes, but I don't want to miss a thing. If her wolf comes back, I want to be there for her. I want to be there for Lizzie every step of the way.

First thing we have to do is tell her we're her mates. I don't know if she'll know what that means or what she remembers from her pack, but I'll figure it all out in time. I've got forever with my mate and today is just the first day. There's no way I'm going to let her deny me. I'm not going to let her, or her wolf, hide from us anymore.

"You tell her yet?" I silently question Caleb as I push the door open. The room looks just like the kind of room I'd expect any typical twentysomething to have. Caleb made sure to get everything set up exactly how it was for them back at their apartment. These girls really love the color pink. It's everywhere with splashes of yellow and the occasional pale shade of teal. Lizzie is still huddled in the cream-colored damask comforter from the guest room. She's right in the middle of her bed with her head resting on her knees, nuzzled into the blanket. She's got her arms wrapped around her legs and she holds on to them like they're her anchor. When she hears my boots thud against the wooden floors, she lifts her head slightly and her red-rimmed, blue eyes peek through her dark, thick lashes at me. The soft movement of her shoulders becomes rigid with fear.

Her eyes dart to the rope in my hands and terror flashes

over her face. Her kissable, pouty lips release a small gasp and she quickly backs away from me, crawling on her hands and knees to the headboard and pushing her side up against it. She wraps her arms around her bent legs and hastily rocks her body, resting her cheek on her knee so she can keep her eyes on me. Her big doe eyes are drenched in panic and tears fall carelessly down her reddened cheeks. She sniffles before swallowing and saying in a small voice, "Please don't."

With his arms crossed, Caleb stands in the corner on my right; the corded muscles in his neck and arms make him look like a rock-solid beast. At least he has a tight smile on his face. Although that's obviously not doing anything to calm her.

"Nah, I figured you'd want to be here." I glance at him and then walk slowly to the edge of the bed. I sit my massive form down and feel the soft bed dip. Our little mate lets out a squeak. Caleb follows me but doesn't sit.

"I tried to sit when you left and she freaked out."

"This'll help her." I see him slightly shake his head in my periphery. *"Just don't get in my way then."*

"Don't fucking make me."

I clench my teeth and ignore him. Our mate hasn't heard a single word of our silent dialogue and I don't want her to think I'm pissed at her. At least I don't think she has.

"I want you to come sit by me." It's a simple request. My words come out as soft as they possibly can. She stops rocking and stares at me for only a moment before burying her head between her knees as she shakes her head in denial. I resist the urge to growl, not at her disobedience, but at the former pricks who did this to her. Instead I pat the bed next to me and calmly repeat myself. "I want you to come sit by me." I look at Caleb and then back to our scared little mouse. "We have something very important to tell you and I want to be able to hold you when you hear it." Caleb's lips turn up at the corners. I don't know if he's trying to force a smile onto his pretty-boy face or whether he's trying to hold one in.

Caleb stalks closer to her and slowly drops to his knees at the foot of the bed. His tall frame hovers over the mattress as he bends to offer his upturned hand to Lizzie. "Come on, baby girl, I want to hold you too. Let's go sit with Dominick." She doesn't even lift her head to meet his eyes. Her blond hair swings across her back as she shakes her head, adamantly refusing our requests.

"*Let's just tell her.*" I hear Caleb's words in my head, but instead of responding silently I continue to speak out loud so our mate can hear.

"I don't want to tell her until I can hold her."

"*Stop being so fucking stubborn.*" He continues his silent conversation.

"*I'm not being stubborn; when I tell her that she's my mate, she needs to be listening. She's not listening to anything we say.*"

"*She is listening; she doesn't want to obey. There's a difference, Dom.*"

"I know there's a difference. She's hearing us, but she's not really listening." I glance back at our terrified mate before looking Caleb in the eyes. *"You want to claim her on the full moon?"* He squirms uncomfortably.

"You know I do. But I don't want to scare her."

"Too late." I speak out loud, but he doesn't follow suit.

His shoulders slump in defeat. *"I don't want to give her a reason to fear us."*

"She already has one." Frustrated with all this pussyfooting around, I question him, "Are you going to help me?" He grits his teeth and clenches his fists, but then he gives me a slight nod. I take a deep breath and crack my knuckles before turning to fully face our mate.

"Hey, Lizzie," I say and stare at the back of her head. She stops moving but doesn't turn to me, and she doesn't respond. I know she's terrified, so it doesn't make me angry—in fact, it's exactly what I expect.

I sigh and say as casually as I can, "If you won't listen, I'm going to have to tie you up, little one." Her breathing hitches, but other than that I get nothing. I'll give her one last chance. "Come here. Come sit next to me so I'll know you'll hear me." I pat the bed and continue to stare at the back of her head.

"How are we doing this?" Her lack of a response gets Caleb to finally relent.

"Well, do you want to get your eyes clawed out or have your nose kicked in?" A small grin plays at his lips.

CHAPTER 15

DEVIN

I place featherlight kisses along Grace's bare neck as she sits perched on the granite countertop of the large island in the center of the kitchen. I don't want to let go of her, but I know she's dying to get back to Lizzie. I breathe out deep and resign myself to feeding her and then taking her to her room. I'm vaguely aware of Dom's and Caleb's anxiety. They must be going to Lizzie, which means our mates' room is set up.

Dom's feelings are more of a painful anxiousness whereas Caleb's are hopeful but tinged with apprehension. I block them out. They don't need me interfering. They'd better come up with a plan soon to tell her that she's their mate. I don't think I can wait like I'd planned to. Keeping this from her is tearing me up inside. It's easy to see when she's overthinking it all. I know the moment I explain it to Grace everything will fall into place for her. Our bond is already strong, as it should be between mates, but she's still holding back and that's a problem I'm unwilling to allow to go on much longer.

She pulls my shirt down her thighs, covering herself from me, and glances around the large kitchen. I could tell she was shocked by how modern her new home is. She probably expected to live in some shack in the woods. I reach for the cheese and butter in the fridge. After spending a year watching her, I know she makes grilled cheese whenever she's stressed. I made sure to stock up on groceries before we went to the offering. I want her to indulge in anything that will offer her comfort. Once she's settled, she'll have all the comfort she's always wanted.

I set the ingredients by the stove and glance back at her as I reach for a pan. She avoids my gaze and bites her lip, nervously looking around the room again. Her eyes linger on the doorway to the hall. Doubt filters into my mind each time her attention focuses on an escape route. I swear to God if she runs from me again, I'll lose my shit. As long as I'm touching her, she seems fine but the moment I step away, it's like our bond doesn't exist. That's an indescribable pain. Doesn't she feel that as well? There's so much I don't know .. all because she's human. This is the first instance in nearly a century for our kind to mate with humans from what I've heard in the whispers from other packs. It's not common, but it's not completely unheard of either.

"What are you looking for, sweetheart?" I keep my voice even. As if I don't know she's thinking about bolting even though it's written all over her face. She peeks up at me through her lashes and meets my gaze head-on. Well that's a good sign at least. I see her noticeably swallow.

"I was keeping an eye out for the ... others." The jealousy is unexpected. My nostrils flare and my breathing picks up in anger. I can't school my expression fast enough. Her gaze drops to the floor and she hunches her shoulders. She doesn't realize it, but she's trying to shield her neck from me. Yet another thing I don't like. It takes far too much effort to compose myself. This isn't what we're told to expect. Especially for an Alpha's mate. Again, doubt lingers.

"Why are you waiting on ... *others*?" I can't say anything else without giving away how pissed off I am and this level of aggression is not for her. Imagining someone else walking in on her like this, and her attention being given to them ... a pack member and not her mate ... dressed as she is ... The fact that Dom and Caleb are sharing their mate has gone to my head. I turn my back to her and put the pan for her goddamn grilled cheese on the stove to heat. I have to work hard not to slam the drawer shut after I grab a butter knife.

"I ... I ..." Her stammering isn't helping to calm me down. "I don't want to see them." My shoulders relax at her admission.

"That's a hell of a lot better than what I was thinking."

I turn back around to face her before I ask with all seriousness, "Are you afraid of them?" She shakes her head "no" while her beautiful hazel eyes meet my gaze. Nodding, at least I know I chose well for who would accompany her when I couldn't. Lev, even if he is younger and less experienced—he's soft where the rest of us aren't, charming and easy to talk to. He has patience where I don't, and more importantly, he'll protect her.

Satisfied, I nod, letting my gaze drift down her body.

She's so fucking gorgeous covered in just my white T-shirt. I have a perfect view of her pale rose nipples through the thin fabric and I'm not sure if they're hard because she's aroused or if she's cold. Maybe it's both. Her bare feet dangle from the counter and her ankles are crossed. She looks so sweet and innocent. The blush that rises to her cheeks proves she's not so innocent as her gaze lingers on my chest, then moves lower. I watch her lick her lips before her eyes meet mine again. My sexy, knowing smirk makes her roll her eyes.

Damn, I love her confidence.

Her eyes dart to the far edge of the counter as the small smile on her lips fades. I follow her line of sight and my brows pinch. I'm not sure if it's my laptop or something else that's caught her attention, but I'd be willing to bet she would do anything now to tell the people in her hometown that she's all right. Which can never happen. Never. There are laws in place and her silence is required.

I flip her grilled cheese before striding across the room and bringing the laptop to her. I don't care if she uses it and I want her to know I trust her. That she has access to everything she desires.

"Go ahead and order those jeans." I smirk at her shocked expression and then give her a stern look so she knows I'm serious. "No social media, though." Focusing again on the sandwich I turn my back to her, but she nods before she leaves my view.

Her buttered bread is perfectly golden and crispy, with the melted cheese dripping down the sides. I smile inwardly. It's just the way she likes it. I'll never admit to her that I practiced making them as soon as I noticed her obsession. The first week, I burned all the ones I tried making. After that, I had to actually study her while she cooked and realized she kept adding butter. No wonder her ass has that tempting curve to it. My dick hardens at the thought of pounding into her against the wall. I stifle my groan.

"I don't have my card ..." Her sweet voice brings me back to reality. Nervousness echoes in her worried statement.

The ceramic plate clinks on the counter and I slip the grilled cheese onto it before taking it to her. Her hazel eyes light up and the most beautiful smile I've ever seen plays at her lips, exposing her perfect white teeth as she immediately picks up her comfort food, not hesitating for a moment. Sometimes she adds salt, so I grab it from the cabinet and set it next to the empty plate. The sandwich occupies both of her hands. "I love grilled cheese." She practically moans the words through a mouthful of sandwich before she realizes she's talking with her mouth full. She blushes and puts a hand up to her mouth. "Sorry," she chokes out once she swallows.

Fucking adorable.

Shaking my head, I admit, "I don't mind." I glance at the screen and see she's picked out her jeans. They're only fifty bucks and I'm honestly shocked. I thought women's clothing was more expensive than men's. "Those are what you want?"

She hesitantly nods her head. "I know Lizzie wants a pair too." Although it's a statement, her meek voice makes it a question.

"Go ahead and order them, choose the first card that comes up, or any of them. Get as many pairs as you'd like." I turn back to the stove and take a look at my own grilled cheese. I burned it. Motherfucker. I don't really care about the damn thing.

"It's important you only use the computer for shopping ... you know that?"

She nods, midbite and drops the late-night meal to the plate. "I imagine there are rules."

All I give her is a nod and then say, "We'll discuss them later." I take a large bite of my sandwich and gesture to the last bit of hers.

"I didn't know werewolves ate real food." I chuckle at her comment and take a bite with my back leaning against the sink so I can face my mate.

My curiosity is piqued. "What did you think we ate?" Even with as much as I have to tell her, I'm curious to hear what the humans think and say. I've heard things, but the truth is always hidden and less obvious.

She shrugs noncommittally. "No clue. I figured since vampires drink blood, and witches eat organs and nasty shit that you would eat ..." she trails off and scrunches up her nose before concluding, "I don't know, raw meat or something."

From the corner of my eye I watch Lev pause at the doorway when he catches sight of Grace perched on the counter. I nod at him, acknowledging his presence and giving him permission to enter. He walks into the kitchen and yawns audibly, obviously in an attempt to make her aware of his presence before he says, "You two are up early." He eyes Grace on his way to the fridge, no doubt wondering what kind of a mood she's in ... and probably wondering if she's struck me again. "Good morning, Grace." He turns his attention to me and says, "Alpha."

The entire pack knows that she hit me and tried to get away from me. Part of me is delighted because I can feel their admiration for her strength and courage; the other part of me wants to sulk at the fact that she denied me. It's embarrassing at the very least, and alarming at the worst. There's so much she doesn't know, but the wolf of a denied mate can't lead a pack. She doesn't realize how much control she has and how much is at stake.

So, striking me ... it's a precedent that can't be set. Lev got to see it firsthand and I still feel ashamed for making her want to run from me. His presence reminds me that I need to talk to her about why she bolted the moment I left her. And more importantly, how it can't happen again. No matter the circumstance.

"You consider this early to be morning?" she asks Lev like he can't be serious. My lips kick up into a smirk at her response. She's confident and relaxed. She fits right in as the Alpha mate.

It was shocking when I found out my mate was human. When I felt her, when I was drawn to her. Having to leave without her at last year's offering was ... excruciating. The pain is inhumane. We're the strongest pack on this side of the country. I thought having a human mate would make me weak and waiting for her certainly held its challenges, but I can already feel the power she's giving me through our bond. I'm honored to be her mate even if she's younger and has so much to learn. I hope one day she'll feel the same way.

Lev smiles at her response after taking a swig from the jug of orange juice. "Well, it's the morning shift." He wipes his mouth with the back of his hand. Lev is ... Lev. A fucking animal. "I've got to go do my laps and get shit in order before

Jude checks out."

Grace tilts her head in confusion, her brunette hair slipping from her shoulder and falling behind her. The curve of her neck is ... tempting.

"We have to do rounds to ensure the estate is secure," he explains to Grace and her expression falls just slightly, a flicker of uncertainty present. As she swallows, her fingers grip the edge of the counter slightly.

"You think ... you think someone would try to come for us?" she questions and Lev keeps his laugh to himself, although I hear it.

"She doesn't need to know yet," I warn Lev and although he doesn't respond to me, he tells her, "No, it's just a good habit for a wolf to be in." We share a glance and Grace's shoulders lose some of their tension. She offers him a tight smile.

"Already lying to her?"

"I'll tell her soon," I answer Lev but then doubt myself and my decision. Never in the years since we've formed a pack have I doubted so much. She brings questions and unease, but it feels right and just.

My pack's on high alert now that the old Alpha has threatened to return. I should've killed him rather than shown mercy. I shake my head and silently tell Lev to shut the fuck up. She doesn't need to know about all that shit. Not after the day she's had.

Grace yawns although it's obvious she tried to hold it

back, and then says, "Well, I call this bedtime." Her shirt rises up as she stretches her arms above her head. The hem tickles her upper thighs, and with the small movement and realization she's only in a top, her eyes widen with a hint of embarrassment. She grabs the fabric and pulls it down as a rosy blush of embarrassment brightens her cheeks. I let a chuckle rumble through my chest. We're shifters, so we don't give a fuck about nudity. I want her to feel comfortable, though.

Lev smirks at her response so I have to silently scold the little shit. *"Have some respect for her modesty, Lev."*

"Sorry, Dev." I hear his humorous remark in my head. He turns on his heels leaving the juice on the counter and heads toward the hall while calling out, "Good night, Grace. See you two later."

Grace calls out in a strained voice, "See you, Lev," while pushing her knees and thighs together and staring at the floor. She whispers, "I'm sorry. I forgot I was only wearing a T-shirt." Her eyes peek up at me, searching for something, and I reach out to cup her chin and run my thumb along her bottom lip.

"It's all right, sweetheart. You don't have to worry about that. Lev doesn't mind." My words don't have the effect I thought they would. She pulls away from my grasp and I let my hand fall to my side. She noticeably swallows.

"I want to go to bed," she speaks quietly to the floor. I can tell she's trying hard not to say something and I have no fucking clue why.

"What's wrong?" She shakes her head, still not making eye contact and I'm not going to stand for that. That's not what this is between us. I should be able to hear everything. Frustration is ... so unexpected. I take her chin in my hand again and force her to look at me. Her skin is hot against mine, sparking from the small contact. My gaze bores into her hazel eyes, willing her to answer. She squares her shoulders before shrugging.

"I'm fine. Really. It's just been a long day." I stare at her lying ass for a few seconds before releasing my hold on her. It only takes a second of debating whether or not I should drop this. She's keeping shit from me, but I'm guilty of doing the same to her. Her hands cover her face for a moment before she lifts her hair off her shoulders, breathes in deep, and exhales slow and steady. She twists the hair at the nape of her neck and pulls her brunette locks over her shoulder.

My eyes focus on the sight of her exposed neck; it's a welcome distraction. There are a few tiny scrapes on her delicate skin from my fangs and it makes my dick hard remembering how I fucked her earlier. The marks call to me to bite her. Hard. To claim her by sinking my fangs deep into her tender, pale flesh. I lean down and run my tongue over the most prominent mark, torturing my wolf. She leans into me and hums in approval. I grin into her neck. I may not be able to justify scolding her for keeping secrets when I am too, but I can give her a merciless, punishing fuck. I nuzzle under her ear before nipping her lobe. Her thick thighs clench together as I smell her arousal.

My intentions were to feed her and then take her to bed, but I can't let her go without satisfying all of her hunger, and my own. I run my fingers down her neck to her collarbone then trail back up as I plant small kisses on the other side, up to that tender spot behind her ear. She shivers at my touch. I fucking love it.

"I know you're tired, sweetheart, but I'm not going to leave you while you're in need." I take her bottom lip in between my teeth and bite down hard enough that it'll leave a bruise. She yelps and her little whimper makes my dick swell with desire. I swiftly pick her up off the counter and lay her on her stomach across the barstool so she's at the perfect height for me to fuck her greedy cunt with long, hard strokes.

Brushing her hair over one shoulder, I grip the nape of her neck. With my chest pressed to her back, I listen to her unsteady breathing pick up. Nothing but lust settles in the warm air between us. She moans my name and arches her back just slightly. This is the obedience I've craved. She's a dream come true. Letting my lips tickle the shell of her ear, I whisper, "Hold on, sweetheart." Her hands instantly grab the legs of the stool while I slam my dick into her.

Fuck, she's even tighter than she was earlier. She's got to be sore to be this swollen and I've only taken her twice so far, but I know that the pain will only heighten her pleasure. The barstool wobbles on the ground, struggling to stay balanced as I hammer my dick into her, pulling almost all the way out and then slamming back in over and over. My grip tightens on her hips as she bites down on her bottom lip, attempting to quiet her sounds of pleasure.

I groan as the feeling of her tight walls stroking my length sends a heated rush through my body, starting at my toes and working its way up in long pulses. She feels too fucking good. I keep my pace slow and steady, knowing how intense it is for her. Hard and fast is right around the corner, but she needs to get off first.

It only takes a few more strokes for me to push her to the edge of her release. Her body trembles and she bites her arm to quiet her moans. I slam my hips into her, forcing her to take all of me and hold it there while she screams out my name and arches her back as her orgasm rips through her body. *Fucking perfect.*

I ride recklessly through her orgasm. My fingers dig into the tender flesh at the front of her throat as I grip her harder. Her arousal makes pistoning into her easier and I pick up my pace, brutally pounding into her welcoming heat. The sound of me fucking her, with her sweet low moans muffled in the background, fuels my need to find my own release. With my left hand gripping her nape to steady her body as I rut into her swollen cunt, I use my right hand to roughly rub her throbbing clit. She struggles beneath me to get away from the intense pressure building in her so soon after her first release. But I want it. I want more of her and all of her.

There's a very sick desire I possess for her to feel me inside of her every second she's away from me.

My hands go numb as a cold sweat breaks out on my skin. The need for release creeps up on my body, slowly building in intensity. I growl into her ear with a primal need, "Come for me." Being so close to her neck makes my fangs ache with the desperate need to mark her and claim her as mine. I let them skim along her sensitive skin, causing a shiver to run down her barely clothed body. My words and the gentle touch of my sharp fangs send her over the edge and I come hard with her. I ride through both of our orgasms as the pleasure numbs my toes and makes my legs tremble.

It's only once she's sated, panting, and limp beneath me that I can breathe again. I lay my chest over her back to plant small kisses over the marks on her neck as my breathing slows with my dick still hard inside her. My arms wrap around her small, limp body and I effortlessly pick her up. I slip out of her as I sit on the barstool and nestle her into my chest then tenderly kiss her forehead. I take my time soothing her, wanting to stay in this moment as the time ticks by. She sighs, happily satisfied, and snuggles against me as she slowly drifts into sleep. I debate on waking her up and fucking her until I've had my fill, but it's late and the sight of her relaxed body in my arms is enough to temper my appetite. For now.

CHAPTER 16

CALEB

Liz continues to furiously struggle beneath my huge form trying to get away from us. I'm doing my best not to bruise her little body, but she's putting up one hell of a fight. I'm ashamed at how much I crave this. I don't enjoy her fear, but the need to punish and condition her? I'm a sick, sadistic fuck for how much I desire just that.

To say I'm projecting on Dom is an understatement. I want to punish our little mate. I want to slam into her tight little ass and rut into her while she screams out in an overwhelming mix of agony and desire. I'll make it feel good for her of course, but there'll be pain. I know she's scared, but that doesn't change my need to prove to her that she belongs to me. That I'm worthy of her and being her mate, and that I can help her. I'm hard just thinking about it. Like I said, I'm a sick fuck. I only hope my little mate has a beast in her that wants to come out and play just as much as mine does.

Dom's plan of action only fuels my desires. Tying her up is our next move. She's going to fight us every step of the way and I desperately want her to challenge me. Knowing she's not human puts me on edge, but in a way that gives me relief. If she were human, I'd have to go easy on her and be careful. I can't hurt my mate. Physically or emotionally. I don't want to either. But fucking her within an inch of her life, I'm dying to do that. Knowing she's got shifter blood in her means she could take more punishment than a human can. I know it's going to be hard to control how rough I am with her. I'll try, but I'm dying with need. Need to let out my inner demon and thrust into her with unforgiving, deep strokes. Need to have her writhing beneath me, trying to get away from the pain yet at the same time needing more of it. It's a cruel, twisted need, but it's a need nonetheless.

And she needs to know she's mine, she's safe and she is wanted more than she could possibly imagine.

I've always had these desires. Slow, sweet, and passionate has never interested me. I need it hard and savage. I've never given my perversions free rein. I've never spoken them out loud or let anyone sense these urges. Seeing my mate refuse me, that makes me want to let loose on her. Let my beast out to ruthlessly claim her for himself. Maybe that's why fate gifted me a mate I'm destined to share with Dom. He's frightening to look at, but he has control where I am lacking. I'm a slave to my beast. I should tell Dom what I want to do to her, but he's so wrapped up in having her forgive him for shit he didn't even do that he hasn't noticed my lust for her body.

I have the look of her tearstained face memorized. I love the way fear and anger look on her because it's evidence of how much she needs me. I want her to scream and cry, letting her tears run freely down her gorgeous face while I punish every inch of her body for denying us. For thinking for one second that she doesn't belong to us. More than that, I desperately need her to fight me. I want to feel her sharp nails dig into my back as I draw out every orgasm I possibly can from her body. The only regret I have is that she won't be able to leave scars. That's a damn shame. I want her marks all over me. And mine all over her.

Liz's nails scrape across my neck while I tie one of her wrists to the headboard and I have to stifle a groan. I can feel her squirming beneath me to get out of Dom's grasp. For being so small she's got a hell of a lot of fight in her. It makes me hopeful. Whatever she went through didn't kill her spirit. All of a sudden, her fist swings out of nowhere and lands square on my jaw.

"Fuck!"

I wrap my hand around her throat knowing her natural

reaction will have her hand flying to my fingers to try and pry them off. I lean back and flex my jaw. It actually hurts. A touch of pain makes me smile inwardly. I tighten the rope on one wrist, making sure it's properly secured while my other hand presses against her small, fragile neck. It's enough pressure to feel the blood pumping through her veins, but I'm not pushing hard enough to actually cut off her breathing. I just want her other hand busy while I make sure I have her where I want her.

"Baby girl, that hurt." I admonish her while grabbing her other wrist in my left hand and the rope in my right. Her eyes widen as she realizes her struggling is useless now. The shadow of Dom standing up behind me catches my attention; he must have secured her legs. She screams out unintelligibly, but within seconds Dom shoves something in her mouth. I glance at her to see what it is. She's shaking her head and trying to spit out his shirt that now acts as a gag. I tug on the rope and fasten it tighter to the bed to restrict her movements as much as possible. I finally breathe out and climb off the mattress to have a look at our gorgeous mate all tied up.

No longer able to fight us, no longer able to hurt herself.

Her dress is bunched up around her waist revealing a cream thong that's begging to be torn from her. It takes every bit of self-control I have not to shove my face in between her legs and leave a languid lick. Her breasts are covered by a simple white strapless bra and I want to rip it to shreds. It's not sexy enough to grace her skin. Our mate is anything but simple. She should be covered in skimpy but expensive lace. My dick hardens at the thought. Or leather. Fuck, she would look so hot with a thin leather strip draped over her breasts, just wide enough to cover her nipples, to tease me. I resist the urge to palm my dick; now is not the time. Not when she's still as scared as she is. Her long platinum blond hair is spread out under her in a messy halo, making her look wild and recently fucked. Damn shame the last part isn't as true as the first. Wild perfectly describes our mate.

That's when I notice the small bruises around her wrist, hips, thighs, and ankles. I stare at them waiting for the purplish blue to slowly fade. They aren't bad, but she's pulling against the rope and it's going to rub her skin raw or give her welts, or both. She needs to knock that shit off and let them heal as wolves do.

"Stop struggling." I give her the command with ease but worry filters in as the bruises appear to darken. "You're going to hurt yourself, baby." She yells something incoherent through the shirt stuffed in her mouth and I have to suppress a grin. The happiness sneaking up on me at seeing our mate spread out for us vanishes when I look back at her bruises. They look even darker. *What the fuck?* I hear Dom thinking the same; she should be healing by now. Concern for our mate rapidly kills any desire I had.

"We hurt her." I shake my head in disgust. Yeah I want to

fuck her and bring her to the edge of pain while I pleasure her delectable body, but I don't want her injured in any other way. She's a wolf. I heard it. Dom heard it. She isn't supposed to be bruised. I don't want to mark her unless she can look at them and remember the pleasure that came with it. This isn't what I want. A deep regret settles in my chest. *"Why isn't she healing?"*

"She's not a werewolf." My neck whips around at Dom's blunt statement.

"The hell she's not; you heard her wolf!" My breathing becomes erratic and adrenaline starts pumping through my blood, making my fists tremble with the need to thrash against something. And right now, Dom's face is looking like the best option.

"Calm down, Caleb. She's going to be fine. Her wolf is in there, but she's something else."

"She needs to heal. Why isn't her wolf healing her?" I don't understand what's happening.

He ignores me, which only intensifies my alarm, speaking his next words aloud so Liz can hear. "Little one, you okay?" I'm pretty sure the two syllables she shouts into his shirt are "Fuck you!" A grin threatens to pull at my lips, but I stop that shit; she's not okay. And I don't know how to handle her if she can't heal herself. How can I be rough with her then? How can I be who I am with my mate if she's unable to take something as simple as this?

"Baby girl, bring your wolf back so she can heal you." I focus on the one thing all of us need. "I don't like seeing these marks on your body." I'm surprised by the absolute truth in that statement. I never thought I'd want her marks to go away but then again, these weren't given to her in the way my wolf demands. She shakes her head violently at my command. My brows knit together in anger at her insolence and Dom's hand comes down on my shoulder in an attempt to placate me.

"Calm the fuck down."

Dom crawls on the bed, making it dip and groan, and straddles her tiny frame while he talks. "I want to talk to you. Are you going to be good so I can take your gag away?" Her eyes travel over his body and I scent the air; there's nothing but fear and anger. My wolf snarls in my chest. I want her arousal. Taking a seat on the edge of the bed, I rub soothing circles on her calf. She flinches at first, but soon resigns herself to my touch. It's not like she's in any position to stop me. Dom looks back at me and his eyes light up as he watches me caress her tender skin.

"Maybe we should keep your gag in until you're more relaxed." He stares into her piercing blue eyes and she stares defiantly right back.

"Baby girl, we have something important to tell you." I trail my fingers teasingly up and down her calf before taking her knee in my hand. I want to kiss her leg, but she'll probably just knee me in the face and break my nose. The motion would take all the slack these ropes have for her to do it, but there's not a doubt in my mind she would, so I hold back.

I share a glance with Dom before continuing to talk to Liz and he nods his head in agreement. Now that she can't ignore us and can't run from us, it's the perfect time to tell her we're her mates. Even if she is spitting mad. Beggars can't be choosers. "Baby, when you were with your pack, did you learn about mates?" I'm reaching here. She may have wolf in her, but I don't have a clue whether or not she was ever in a pack. Her body tenses at my question. I press my lips in a hard line. Damn it. I want her to relax.

"You shouldn't have brought up her pack." Dom silently scolds me.

"Then you fucking do it." I answer him in my head so that she doesn't hear my irritation.

"Lizzie, we're your mates." Dom makes the matter-of-fact statement while he bends down to pick up more rope. I scrunch up my face and hang my head at his nonchalance.

"What the fuck, Dom?"

"What?" He looks at me like he's confused as to why I would be aggravated.

"Women want romance, you dumb fuck." I hiss the words in my head.

"Does she look like she wants romance right now?" I take a look at my doe-eyed mate. She's still scared to death and furious, looking at Dom like he just smacked her across her pretty little face. *"She's not even listening. Look at her."*

"Do you know what that means, Liz? That we're your

mates?" I ask her evenly, making my voice as soft as I possibly can even though the words choke me. I expect her to shake or nod her head, but she does nothing. I school my expression to keep my anger under wraps.

"She really likes being difficult, doesn't she?"

"It'll take time, but we'll break her habit of ignoring us."

Dom's words ring clear in my head. I don't respond because truthfully I want her to be difficult so we can let our beasts out to play. But not right now. Not when I'm telling her that she's my one and only for as long as I live. That she is my everything and every choice I make will involve her and prioritize her. My heart clenches and my hand stills on her calf. Fuck. Maybe fate knew how fucked up I'd end up being so they gave me a mate who can't love me back. I have to clear my throat and stop those thoughts. I'll *make* her love me.

"Nod if you understand." She stares back defiantly although some of her fight has waned.

"We're your mates. You belong to us and we belong to you." Dom's statement means more to me than anything else I've ever heard.

She hears, she knows. I know she does from the way her breathing picks up and her chest rises and falls heavily. It's sinking in and I pray she can feel the pull and how much stronger it's gotten in only seconds.

"Do you understand what that means? That we're both your mates and you are our only?"

"Little one, answer Caleb." Dom's voice is level, but full of authority. Our stubborn mate continues to ignore the two of us, refusing to nod or attempt to speak. But I know she heard; I know it's dawning on her. Dom sighs as though he's not looking forward to what he's about to do and I watch as he crawls on the bed to wind rope around her knee that's farthest from me. After he knots it, he pulls it to the edge of the bed, forcing her legs to spread apart. He secures the rope to something under the bed and I can't help but wonder where he came up with this idea. My dick pulses in agony at the sight of her legs being forced open. She's completely exposed with no way to hide and I fucking love it.

"You're my mate, Lizzie. *Our* mate." He glances at me and I nod my head while keeping my eyes on Liz. She looks downright pathetic as she struggles against the rope at her knee. I use a little force to bring her other knee up while Dom secures it. I can't take my eyes off of her pussy. The skimpy lace has shifted from her struggles and she's partially exposed. My mouth waters at the sight. Dom moves between her legs then gently pets her pussy, and the smell of her desire nearly makes me lose all control. Between fear and lust, a being will cling to lust. It's just a matter of offering it, and letting them choose it willingly.

"We're going to relax you, Lizzie," he says as he rubs his thumb along her clit. I see him press down as he looks back up at Liz to gauge her reaction. "I won't fuck you until you beg me." She moans and throws her head back at his touch.

making my dick struggle for release in my pants.

"You'll snap your fingers if it's too much," he says, allowing her a safe signal and Liz's only response is to breathe in deeply. "Do it once for me," he commands her. When she doesn't answer, he pauses his ministrations. I nearly repeat his demand, desperate for this to continue, but she looks him dead in the eye and her fingers come together, although there's no crisp snap. She makes the effort and that's good enough for him.

I watch as two of his thick fingers slip past the lace material and dip into her heat. His thumb continues to rub circles against her little nub while he strokes the front wall of her pussy, hitting that sweet spot that has her nearly begging for more.

"Fuck, you're tight." He finger fucks her harder. I groan at the sight of her writhing helplessly at his touch. I lean down and kiss the inside of her knee as a reward for her. I grin as I realize even if she wanted to bash my nose in with her knee, she couldn't. She can barely move any part of her body. Liz moans and rocks her pussy against Dom's hand as she gets closer and closer to her release. She's pulling at her ropes, but this time it's not to escape.

"Caleb asked you a question, little one." He stops all of his movements and looks expectantly at her. Her eyes pop open, revealing dilated pupils and she hisses something at him through the shirt.

"Do you know what it means to be our mate?" he asks her calmly.

She nods vigorously. "Good girl." He starts hammering his fingers into her cunt, adding a third, and leans down to suck her clit into his mouth. Her moans of pleasure fuel my need to be inside her and I struggle to keep my eyes from closing in ecstasy. I don't want to miss seeing any second of Dom coaxing her orgasm out of her. All I can smell is her arousal and it's suffocating me. I give in to my need to find my release and stand up, unzipping my pants while watching my gorgeous mate writhe with pleasure.

"I want to fuck you, baby. Tell me I can fuck you." Although it's meant to be a command, I'm practically begging as I pant out the words. Even as she's approaching her climax, she shakes her head, refusing my need for her welcoming heat. I groan out in agony as I climb on the bed. "That's all right, baby. I understand." I stroke myself over her and breathe heavily as my spine tingles and my toes go numb. The gag is muffling her sounds too much and I need to hear her just a little more clearly as I race for my own release. I rip the shirt out of her mouth and she screams out in ecstasy, thrashing her head as she comes all over Dom's fingers. Just the sight of her screaming in pleasure pushes me over the edge.

As my breathing calms down, I hear Dom's pick up.

"Eat her pussy, Caleb." I only pause for a second at the command. Then I see the desperate look of lust in his eyes and I don't hesitate to scoot down her body. I got mine. Now he needs to get his.

CHAPTER 17

LIZZIE

I'm just barely coming down from the most intense orgasm I've ever had, when I feel Caleb's hot tongue licking up my arousal that's leaking down my thighs. His tongue dives into my heat, causing me to arch my back with what little freedom I have to move.

"Yes!" I buck my hips, pushing myself into his face, needing more. He ravishes me like a starving man. I'm vaguely aware of Dom kneeling over my stomach. I'm able to glance down and my eyes widen as I watch him pleasure himself. His large hand is barely able to wrap around it. He's far too large. I start to shake my head, but before I can think too much, Caleb bites my clit. Hard. I cry out in a mix of intense pain and pleasure.

"You want more, baby girl?" I don't waste a single second to nod. *Yes*! Yes, I want more. He sucks my clit while his fingers thrust deeper and deeper inside me, stroking my front wall each time. Hitting that rough spot that has me begging for his touch. I'm so damn sensitive to every small movement he makes. My body is pulling to get away, but at the same time pushing to get closer.

"Fuck, Dom, she's still got her cherry for us."

Dom leans back and I watch him stroke himself to climax at the realization that I'm still a virgin. He spurts his release all over my chest while he groans a rough, low moan. It's the sexiest fucking thing I've ever seen. I can't look into his eyes, though. I can't bring myself to do it.

Mates. They are my mates. It's cruel really. Fate is cruel.

I watch as Caleb licks my arousal from his lips while staring at me with the forceful hunger of a brute. I can't deny I'm attracted to them. My body absolutely is. And my mind is soothed hearing the word *mate*.

Still, if I weren't tied down, I would run. I can't help it.

"Are you more relaxed now?" Dom asks and I nod once, letting my eyes close. Betrayal seeps into my veins. So much of it, for so many reasons.

I don't know which one of them is sexier. The rough savage who's kneading my breasts and plucking my nipples crudely between his knuckles, or the skilled huntsman who's flicking his tongue along my throbbing, hot clit. I writhe and moan as they attack my body in unison.

"Come on Caleb's tongue like a good girl." Dom's dirty words bring me to the edge of another release. "Come for your mates."

My mates. My pussy clenches and another orgasm tears through my body. Waves of heat run over my skin as I scream out my release, lighting a flame that I didn't know existed inside of me. I breathe heavily, my chest rising and falling sporadically. I'm barely able to lift my head to meet Dom's. His soft, smooth lips crash onto mine. His tongue dives into my mouth and I run my tongue along his. Caleb nips my collarbone, leaving a hot stinging pulse where his teeth marked me and I break away from Dom's kiss to meet Caleb's waiting lips. Blood rushes loudly in my ears as I struggle to stay awake. *My mates.*

I hear a door creak open and my mates shift their attention from me to whomever just came in.

I can't look at them. Whoever it is ... I can barely deal with myself. Let alone my mates ...

Part V

The
Claiming

CHAPTER 18

GRACE

I pound my white-knuckled fists against Devin's solid, chiseled chest. A low growl tears through his throat, but I don't care. A small part of me knows this is stupid because I'm pissing off a beast who could easily crush me. Another, much larger part of me knows it's stupid because I'm only going to hurt myself; his body isn't reacting at all even though I put every ounce of strength into each blow.

He swore to me. He promised. And what I just saw is horrific. How fucking dare they! I would scream but his hand is over my mouth, his arm wrapped around me, trapping me, preventing me from going to her.

They tied her up. They took from her. I swear to God I'll

kill them.

I ignore the voices screaming in my head for me to stop.

My breathing hitches as I recall the sight of those two monsters hovering over her small body. My body is weak and my efforts useless. Tears stream down my hot red face in wretched anger as I put every bit of energy I can muster behind what little resistance I can manage. My breathing is shallow and desperate. I'm vaguely registering his command for me to stop, but I don't pay his words any attention. He saw and did nothing! I hear him yell louder but again, I ignore his demand. My only need is to get back to Lizzie.

I swear I try. I do everything I can, including scratching and biting, the last resorts I have. Nothing seems to affect him.

I attempt to push past his massive frame to get to her. I scream out her name, but Devin's large hand covers my mouth again, silencing my call for her. A growl of my own rumbles in my chest as I open my mouth in an attempt to bite him. He sees my attack coming and forces my head back causing me to stumble, banging my shoulders and back against the wall. One hand pins my wrists above my head and the other has a firm grasp on my chin and mouth, effectively silencing me.

"This isn't the first time I've let you hit me, sweetheart." Devin's sneered words at the shell of my ear are dripping with menace. His warm breath on my neck sends a wanton heat rushing through me. Tears well in my eyes. I hate my treacherous body; I hate him. I hate all of this. "But it's the last time I'll let you get away with it."

"Fuck you!" I scream at him, unbothered by his tone. My body shakes with tremors from fear, but I don't care anymore. I thought ... I can't even say out loud what I thought I felt for him. How could I be so stupid? My body pleads with me for his touch, to rub against him and beg for forgiveness. I won't do it. I won't lower myself to this pathetic "heat." I'd rather die than let them hurt her.

His hard erection digs into my stomach as he presses his body against mine. A whimper is forced from my lips and I wish I could take it back. I don't want him to affect me. I don't want to give him the pleasure of knowing he can affect me. A sob heaves up my throat. *Lizzie.* My body goes limp in his hold. I've failed her. Another sob wracks through me. There's nothing I can do to help her.

How could they hurt her? How could they do that to her?

"They're her mates; they won't hurt her." His authoritative declaration echoes in my ears. I'm overwhelmed with self-loathing and hatred that I fail to register his words. I let the tears fall freely and stare at the rug lining the wood floors of the hall.

"Look at me!" His demand shoots through my body with an inhuman force. Immediately my eyes find his. Sadness grips me harder than he does. If he fails to see that, it's his own demise.

His silver eyes penetrate mine with a power that makes me want to bow to him, but I won't fucking do it. I stare back with hatred and defiance. He breathes in deep as he relaxes his hold on my chin. I don't take my eyes off of his, and somehow the piercing silver of his gaze softens. It's subtle. He's still a dominating brute, a powerful force not meant to be denied, but somehow diminished. The sickening churning of my stomach lessens slightly, but his eyes still hold a command.

"Listen to me." Although his words are harshly spoken with barely restrained anger, I hear desperation in his voice for me to obey him. I continue to stare into his eyes, relaying my decision to give him my attention. Even if my fists have yet to relax, the skin tight across my knuckles.

"They're her mates. They love her and won't do anything to hurt her." I part my lips to utter my disagreement with his explanation but his eyes narrow, warning me. I'm tempted to push him. *Go ahead and hurt me; show me who you really are!* My heart clenches in agony and my throat closes at the thought. His hand gentles against my throat and his thumb rubs against the line of my jaw. I close my eyes and enjoy his touch for a moment. Just one. Only one moment to feel his caring devotion.

"Come watch, but you *will* keep your mouth shut." He growls his command in my ear and it cracks the bit of peace I'd hidden behind in that small moment. My anger comes back with a heaving breath. As I part my lips to berate him, Devin jams his thumb into my rebellious mouth, scraping his skin along my teeth, once again silencing me. The force of his hand shoves my head against the wall. A snarl forces its way past my lips and I sink my teeth deeper into his flesh while my eyes narrow in a threat.

"Go ahead and bite me." His eyes meet mine. "I won't interfere with the way they handle their mate. For the first time since she's been here, she's relaxed and content." His words settle in me as I let them burrow into my head.

Mates.

"They are devoted to her. Caleb and Dom will be by her side however she needs. And if this is how it had to happen ... then it's how it happened and you will not harm them."

My pulse flickers. Harm them? But more than that, mates? *Mates.* The word resonates deeply.

It's hard to weigh the truth in his statement. The moment I saw her tied to the bed with Caleb and Dom surrounding her, Devin snatched me away, leaving only a blip of an image rattling in my memory. I shake my head. She wouldn't do that. There's no way she would've wanted it.

"If she'd seen us earlier, do you think she would've realized what was going on between the two of us?" he asks as though he read my mind.

"If she walked in on us while I had you against the wall, would she have known how much you fucking loved it? How you wanted me to pin you down and hammer into your hot cunt to prove you belong to me?" My breathing hitches as his dirty words are whispered into my neck, just before he gives it a gentle kiss. The softness of his touch is at odds with his tone, but I cling to it.

"Look at me." His command is softly spoken, nearly a whisper. I tilt my head as he removes his hold on me altogether and steps back. My body instantly misses his warmth, his touch. I want what he's saying to be true. It means they didn't hurt her. Please, God, I want that to be true.

"I want you to see." It takes a moment for me to register his words and I have to blink away the hazy desire clouding my vision, my thoughts, my self-respect. I hate this. I hate this damned heat. I hate the effect he has on me. Anger rips through me. Devin pinches my chin, forcing my eyes to focus on his. I clench my teeth but stare back into his heated silver gaze.

His eyes search mine for a moment before he releases his hold. "Come with me." He walks toward the door without waiting for my response, leaving me to watch his hulking frame take long, confident strides to the door before quietly opening it. My feet hesitantly follow without my conscious consent. I swallow thickly as I realize I'm not sure I want to see. As I come up behind him, he angles his body toward me and opens his arms for me to stand at his side. I glance up at his stern expression and question whether or not I want to be in his embrace. I'm not given the opportunity to deny him as my body continues to behave of its own accord, moving next to him. I close my eyes as his strong arm wraps around my body. His hand rests on my shoulder and his thumb kneads soothing circles into my tense muscles. He peers into the room with me. I close my eyes, reveling in his comforting touch. "Stay quiet, I don't want to interfere. Do you understand?" I nod my head slightly and whisper yes before focusing my gaze on the sight of the three of them. My eyes slowly adjust to the darkened room, illuminated with only hints of daylight whispering through the curtains.

My body stiffens as I watch Dom wipe Lizzie's lower half clean. Before getting off the bed, he places a small kiss on her inner thigh. Caleb is lying next to her on her left but leaning his massive chest over her small frame, loosening a knot on her wrist. He tosses the rope onto the floor and then massages her arm. She turns so her chest is beside his and he responds by pulling her small body against him. My breathing slows and I relax slightly into Devin's hold.

Thump, thump, my heart pleads for this to unfold in a way that will make it all okay.

Dom walks to the other side, releasing her other wrist before climbing onto the bed to lay behind her, his chest to her back. He gently kisses her shoulder and runs his hand over a bruise on her hip. My lungs halt as I see the marks on her body. Her ankles are red and look raw. I shake my head and try to back away, but Devin holds me steady. "Just listen."

"Please bring your wolf out. You're hurt." Dom's whispered plea is almost too soft to hear. *Wolf?* My brow furrows in confusion. Before I can whisper that she's not a wolf, she speaks.

"I can't." I hear Lizzie for the first time and naturally I try to step forward to call out her name, but Devin's strong grip keeps me by his side. My instinct is to push him away so I can go to her, but he holds me in place.

"Could you try?" Dom's words sound wounded and desperate.

A small sob escapes her as she shakes her head into Caleb's chest. "It's okay, baby girl. We'll take care of you. Just relax. You're safe now." Caleb places his head on top of hers while Dom nuzzles into her neck before kissing her sweetly.

"Hold me." I can barely hear her.

"We're here, baby girl." I watch as Caleb strokes her cheek with care before wrapping his arms around her.

"Sleep, little one." Dom covers their bodies with a cream-colored damask comforter before getting back into position, molding his muscular body against hers.

I can't stop staring at the three of them. Even as Devin closes the door, I continue to stare straight ahead, unable to blink away the sight of their loving touch.

"She's their mate. I told you they wouldn't hurt her." He turns me to face him and stares into my hazel eyes. "They may have to push her. She's in a lot of pain. But they aren't going to hurt her. I promise you."

As Devin leads me away from their room, I steady my breathing and try to come to terms with his words. So many thoughts and emotions threaten to overwhelm me. Relief and confusion are the two winning out.

"She's a werewolf?" I don't even realize that I've spoken until Devin stops at a massive door at the far end of the long hall and forces my body to turn to face his.

"She's the same woman you grew up with. She's your best friend. Don't think too much on what you heard. You'll have a chance to talk to her tomorrow." I nod my head in agreement and blink my sore eyes.

"And they love her, like really love her?" Devin gives me the most handsome, genuine smile.

"They do. She's their mate." His eyes are soft and his smile lingers on his lips. I can practically feel his happiness and it warms my heart. "They would die for her."

His hand spears into my hair and I lean into his touch. "And Grace?"

"Hmm?" I open my eyes and find his soft, yet heated silver gaze on me.

"You're my mate." Hearing those words on his lips awakens something deep inside of me, numbing every pain and settling every doubt I've clung to, lighting them to fuel a fire of need. His lips find mine as he walks me backward into his room and kicks the door closed without breaking our contact. His hands fondle my ass before lifting me up into his chest. I wrap my legs tight around his hips and moan into his mouth as he deepens the kiss.

"Mate." He growls the word before nipping my bottom lip, fanning that fire in my core and sending desire pulsing through every inch of me.

CHAPTER 19

GRACE

"I can't wait to claim you with my mark," he says as his pointer finger lightly skims along the tender skin of my neck, "here."

"Your mark?" My half-lidded eyes close, loving his touch.

An asymmetric grin pulls at his lips, exposing one of his sharp fangs. "My bite. It'll scar you and you'll forever be marked as my mate."

There's a mixed concoction of both desire and fear at the thought of his fangs piercing my flesh. I subconsciously arch my neck, offering myself to him. Wanting it more than anything else. His low, rough chuckle rumbles through his chest. "Not now, my love." *Love.* My hopeful eyes find his and he gives me a soft smile. "I love you, Grace. I've loved you for longer than you've known I existed." His admission makes my heart beat erratically, banging wildly against my chest. His strong hold makes me feel safe and secure.

It's a feeling I'm not used to, but it feels like home.

"I love your Alpha spirit." He gently tucks a strand of my hair behind my ear before setting me down. "You have no idea how proud I am to have you as my mate." He takes both of my small wrists in his large hands; seeing the difference in size makes me feel fragile and easily breakable. He kisses the underside of my right wrist and says, "I love your strength and courage." He moves my hand so that my palm rests against the stubble of his strong jaw as he closes his eyes and rubs into my soft, warm touch. "When it's just the two of us, I don't want you to hold anything back from me."

I nod my head and say, "I won't." My immediate agreement makes him smile and he closes his eyes, then leans down to nuzzle his nose along mine.

"I have no doubt of that," he comments.

He breathes in deep before straightening his shoulders and looking down on me with those piercing silver eyes. "It's a different story when we're with the pack, or anywhere that's not private." My eyes instinctively narrow. "If you question me, or if you fight me, then others will target me and the pack. My dominance will be challenged. For the most part, you won't have to worry about anything; just be yourself. But sometimes I'm going to need something from you, sweetheart." His soft, calming tone slowly takes an authoritative edge.

"What's that?"

"Your complete and immediate obedience."

I part my lips to object, but he shakes his head and narrows his eyes. His expression is one of absolute authority. He will not be denied. I struggle with the need to fight him.

"When we're in public, you will listen to me." I hold his gaze with mine, tasting his words on my tongue and not liking them. His brow arches, pushing me for an answer.

"I will try to listen." He immediately narrows his gaze at my honest response.

"No, you *will* listen to me." He gently wraps his hand around the nape of my neck and rubs his thumb over the front of my throat in an unexpectedly soothing way. There's not an ounce of threat in his touch. "There will be times when you're confused, when you don't understand what's going on." His eyes travel from my throat to my eyes. "Even if you think you do, you won't. You'll want to question me, but you won't." There's a finality in his statements. "Do you understand?"

"Yes."

"I'll never do anything to break your trust." His voice softens as his hand caresses my sensitive skin. "Your safety and happiness are at the forefront of every decision I make." I nod my head in the silence between us, acknowledging his words. "Do you believe me?"

His question catches me off guard. My eyes fall to the floor beneath us before reaching his gaze again.

I look deep into his silver eyes; I remember his touch, his words, his looks of devotion. *Mate.* I'm reminded of the shift deep in my soul when he told me I was his mate. I feel an innate sense of comfort and protection with him. He will be my downfall regardless. My soul is very aware of that.

"I do."

He leans down and I push forward, seeking his mouth. Licking and kneading his soft lips with mine. When I pull back, all I can see in his eyes is lust.

"I want you on your knees," he says as his fingers tease my sensitive skin, slowly playing with the hem of my shirt, "now." His commanding voice forces my legs out from under me and I land hard on my knees in front of him as my heated core begs for his attention. *Complete and immediate obedience.*

"Do you like it?" His deep voice is one of control, but he can't hide his desire.

"Do you like me like this?" I try to keep my voice even and leave out my distaste for being wanted to submit as I turn his question on him.

He takes my chin in his hand and tilts it upward, so I'm forced to look into his eyes as he says, "You have no idea what seeing you on your knees does to me." He kisses my lips, licking along the seam and nipping at my bottom lip for me to part for him. I obey, loving his touch and wanting more of it. I feel his passion as his hand fists in my hair and he pulls to cause a hint of pain. I open my mouth to gasp, but I'm silenced as his tongue finds mine in a dark, heated dance. I moan into his mouth as a shot of craving heats my core.

"I have no desire to control you." He breathes heavily as his forehead rests against mine. "Never. I don't want to tame you. But the idea that you'll do what I say simply because I ask? I don't even have the words to describe how much I fucking crave it. Only because it's you." My breath leaves me as I revel in his confession. His lips find mine again and I lean into him, tasting him. His hand fists in my hair again as he takes control of the kiss. He worships my mouth with his tongue.

He slowly stands, leaving me panting and wanting to claw at his pants to get to him. But I know not to. I'm on my knees for him. I wait with bated breath for his instructions as he palms himself.

It's the first time I get a good look at his cock. It's fucking beautiful. I lick my lips at the sight of the thick veins running along his length. He's so big I'm surprised he fit inside me. "Open." My lips part and I open wide to accommodate him as he slides the head of his dick into my mouth.

The feel of his soft, velvety skin on my tongue makes me moan. I run the tip of my tongue along his slit, and he responds by letting out a low hiss. He pushes more of his hard length in my mouth and I greedily accept. I suck him down eagerly, hollowing my cheeks. "Fuck, you're so damn gorgeous," he groans as he pushes his cock deeper. I moan around him as I hear his breathing pick up. I pull back slightly and his silver eyes penetrate mine with a force that makes my pussy beg for his touch.

"I want to touch you." I barely breathe out the words as my desire for him numbs my body.

"Then touch me." My hands instantly wrap around his thick cock and my lips seal around him as I take his length all the way. He fists my hair and shoves himself down my throat.

"Look at me." My eyes instantly find his lustful gaze and the moment they do he releases his hot cum in the back of my throat as his legs tremble, and all the while his silver eyes stay locked on mine. I keep my eyes open, not wanting to break the contact as I swallow him down. He pumps in and out of my mouth in short, shallow thrusts before pulling away from my lips.

His strong arms lift me off the floor and he effortlessly carries me to the bed and tosses me down on the mattress, stalking on his knees toward me. "Open your legs." I obey his simple command, parting them wide as he pushes my thighs apart and he positions himself between them. His hot tongue runs between my legs, lapping up my arousal before flicking my swollen clit.

My back arches and my hands grab his hair, pushing him into me as I moan at the teasing touch. He sucks my clit into his mouth, massaging his tongue against it. "Yes!" I scream out as the pulsing heat runs through my body. My heels dig into the mattress and I push myself harder against him, searching for my release. He pulls back as his fingers continue to tease me, and his eyes focus on my wanting heat.

"Please fuck me," I moan into the hot air.

"You're too sore." He curls his thick fingers, finding that rough spot along my front wall and strokes it mercilessly before leaning down to nibble at my clit.

I claw at his shoulders and scream in desperation for him to pound into me. I feel so empty without him; I know I need him inside me. He smacks my clit with his other hand, causing my body to jolt off of the bed. I scream his name as waves of heated pleasure pulse through my body. Wave after wave keep me trembling as he continues his rough strokes. He slowly pulls out as the aftershocks dim and my breathing steadies.

"Watching you get off is the most beautiful thing I've ever seen," he says then climbs up my body, leaving kisses on my heated skin as he travels to my neck to suck the spot he told me he would bite when he claims me.

"Mmm," is the only response I can manage.

CHAPTER 20

LIZZIE

"You going to fight me again, little one?" My eyelids slowly open to the sound of Dom's rough baritone voice. My loosely closed fists rub my eyes, but they're so damn hot and sore from crying that I have to press my palms into them for relief. The stinging ache only subsides for a moment before I force my hands away and open my eyes to stare back at the two werewolves in the room. My eyes alternate focus between my two mates.

When I see Dom's serious expression, my body instantly recoils. My shoulders hunch and I pull up my legs, wrapping the soft, thick comforter tightly around my body. Shame washes over me, but I can't help my body's reaction. I know he's my mate, but my heart hasn't accepted what my mind has come to terms with. Or maybe it's vice versa; I can't tell. His bulky shoulders rise with his heavy intake of air. The sight of his anger forces a strangled whimper from my throat. I forcefully swallow as I remember his question. "No," I whisper. I won't fight him anymore. Not intentionally, but I can't stop my defensive reactions.

"I'm not going to hurt you." My chest aches at his soft words.

I keep my head hung low as I reply, "I know." He's my mate, and I know everything that the word means. I used to dream of the day, but that was before my life turned into a nightmare.

I listen to them both approach and feel a dip as they sit on the left side of the bed. I lift my eyes to find both of them watching me expectantly. My handsome hunter and gorgeous savage are an intimidating pair. I smile weakly at them, feeling both unworthy and grateful. In truth, I'm relieved to find my mates, but sadness overrides that relief. I'm all too aware of how hollow my chest feels. I know that as their mate, I'm supposed to feel a pull to them. I'm supposed to desire their touch. And I do, but it's subdued. It's so weak I can barely feel the gentle pull. Dom slowly reaches for me with his hand turned upward. I breathe in deep and put my hand in his; it's so small in comparison. His large fingers wrap around my hand and pull me to him. I willingly prop myself up on my knees and silently crawl in between my mates.

They must hate that they're stuck with me. That fate

gifted them such a fragile and broken mate.

I wish I could be better for them. If I could change, I would.

"You going to let us claim you, baby girl?" I nod at Caleb's question as my eyes focus on his gorgeous body. Both men are only wearing jeans. My mouth waters at the sight of their broad bare chests. I may not feel the electric pull I'm supposed to, but I'm still a hot-blooded woman. My eyes roam their bodies shamelessly as my own heats in desire.

"Are you going to accept our marks and both of us as your mates?"

I nod my head and let out an easy sigh. "Yes." I watch as Dom shifts under my gaze and palms his growing erection through his jeans. I love that my gaze of lust is enough to make him want me. It brings a heated blush to my cheeks and a small smile to my lips.

"You know we have to take you to claim you? We have to fuck you and scar you with our bites." Caleb's words draw my attention to him.

I swallow as my thighs clench at the thought and nod my head. "Yes." I never thought I'd be claimed. Why would I, when my wolf has never showed herself. Until last night, when they told me they were my mates, I hadn't realized how badly I wanted it still.

"Come here, I want to taste you." I scoot my body closer to Caleb, my hunter, and offer my mouth to him. His soft lips press against mine. His tongue licks along the seam and I instantly part for him. His strong hand grips my hip and pulls me closer to him. I feel Dom's hand run along my shoulder and slowly grip my nape. As his fingers close around my neck, I break my kiss from Caleb and turn to Dom. Caleb nestles his head in the crook of my neck and gently sucks my sensitive skin.

I moan from Caleb's sweet touch as Dom's teeth nip my bottom lip. My blue eyes find his silver gaze and I nearly crumble from the look of utter devotion. I lean into his lips and his tongue dives into my warm mouth, exploring and tasting with his savage hunger. I hear Caleb unzip his pants as his teeth bite down on my tender earlobe. I moan into Dom's mouth as Caleb climbs behind me on the bed before pulling me away from Dom and into his naked lap, his hard erection digging into the curve of my backside.

My breath comes in short pants as I crane my head to look into Caleb's hard silver eyes. As I do, his hands travel to my breasts, roughly kneading them before pinching my nipples. His gaze holds mine the entire time and I gasp as the pain shoots a heated pulse to my core, dampening my entrance with arousal.

"You like that, baby girl?"

I whimper as his deft fingers pinch my nipples again and let my head fall back onto his shoulder in desire. I barely whisper to the ceiling, "Yes." Dom kisses the front of my exposed throat as his naked body settles in front of me on the bed. My eyes travel from his massive erection up his bulky muscles, to his heated gaze. I swallow as my body starts to shake, overwhelmed with a mix of fear and lust. I fail to steady my hands as Dom reaches for them. *Fuck.* Adrenaline spikes through my blood as my breathing hitches. I wish I could stop this. I wish I could stop my body from fearing him. It's all too obvious he's not the man who haunted my dreams. But the scars are just too deep. Even the smallest hints of the past cripple me. I let him take both of my hands in his and try to steady my breathing. He kisses the knuckles on each hand while rubbing soothing circles against my pulse.

I close my eyes as stray tears travel gently down my cheeks. I'm ashamed at my response to my mates. Caleb licks away the tears. He kisses my hair and whispers, "You're all right. You're here with us. We'll take care of you." I choke out a sob as my forehead lands on Dom's chest. Caleb's strong arms circle tightly around my waist as Dom's wrap around my shoulders. They both whisper calming, loving words, but I can barely hear them. My blood rushes in my ears and the sound drowns out everything else. Caleb and Dom lay me down on my side, keeping their hot, hard bodies pressed against mine.

"Please love me," I gasp.

"We do, little one."

I shake my head against his chest and rock my pussy against his thigh. "No. Like this. Please. Please take the pain away," I beg helplessly into his chest.

"No." He denies me, saying, "Not like this." My tears fall recklessly onto Dom's chest.

"Please. I need you two." A warmth flows through my body as Caleb nibbles my neck and Dom's hand cups my bare pussy. "Yes."

"We'll take care of you," Dom whispers at my lips before taking them with his own. Caleb's fingers travel along the curve of my hips as I rub my sensitive, hardened nipples into Dom's chest and push my ass into Caleb's hips.

I moan into Dom's mouth, "Please." I need this from them. I've never dealt with the past. I've never wanted to. I don't have a choice now, but I just can't take the overwhelming sadness crushing my chest. I need their touch. I need to *feel* something other than fear. Their desire can be that something. I want to feel all-consuming pleasure. Caleb nestles his dick deeper against my ass and gently rocks into me. I moan louder, feeling it vibrate in my chest as Dom rubs the head of his cock on my clit before burrowing it against my folds, grinding into me at a steady pace.

The feel of both of them taking pleasure from my body, both dangerously close to taking my virginity, makes me dizzy with desire.

"Please," I beg as my head spins with a hot, burning need for release. My arousal eases their movements as they rock faster. Even without either of them in me, I feel unbelievably full as Dom's dick assaults my clit and Caleb's rubs against my forbidden ring. They thrust faster, as if they're fucking me, yet I'm achingly empty. Feeling their need to reach their own climax steals my breath. I breathe in hot, heavy air as a cold sweat breaks out along my skin. Dom grips my hip harder and Caleb pulls my thigh tighter to him as they thrust in unison. Caleb kisses my neck while Dom does the same to my breasts, sucking my nipples before pulling them between his teeth.

Their hands roam over my body, gripping and caressing and pulling at me with a desperate need. It's all-consuming, as if they're everywhere at once. I arch my back and wrap my arms around Dom's neck, screaming my pleasure into my bite, while Caleb nearly slips inside of me, and I come violently in their arms. My body trembles with waves of heat burning through me as they both find their release, the three of us peaking in unison. I breathe heavily as the tremors subside.

"I love you, Lizzie."

"I love you too, Liz." They declare their love for me into the hot air between us before leaving kisses in my damp hair and on my forehead.

I hear their words of devotion and I desperately want to feel the same way, but in this moment, I can't say the words back, because I refuse to lie to my mates. A piece of my heart is gone and I just can't let them in to something that's so broken.

"One day you'll say it back to us, but before that day comes, I want you to cry for me, Liz. I want you to pour yourself out to me completely."

"And I want you to shift for me. I don't want any part of you hidden from me."

I nod into Dom's chest while squeezing Caleb's strong hand, silently praying for that day to come.

There is so much more to come in this world. More pieces to be laid out and new stories to unveil now that fate has been set in motion. Wounded Kiss is the first story in the To Be Claimed saga. Gentle Scars, book 2, is up next.

About the Author

Thank you so much for reading my romances. I'm just a stay at home Mom and an avid reader turned Author and I couldn't be happier.

I hope you love my books as much as I do!

More by Willow Winters
www.willowwinterswrites.com/books